A CHRISTMAS VOW

ASTER RIDGE RANCH | BOOK 6

KATE CONDIE

To anyone who has lost themselves

1

EDNA CLIMBED FROM THE COACH, staring wide-eyed at this wind-swept valley she'd run away to. She pressed her fists into her back, tight from the long ride from Billings, and stretched her jaw, tight from forced smiles. She'd rather walk to Billings than face that coach ride one more time. Perhaps that was a good thing, for if her resolve ever faltered, she'd have a day's hard coach ride and another day's train ride just to get back to Chicago. Perhaps if she was ever weak enough to try it, she would have plenty of time to change her mind before returning. To Chicago and to Brandon.

Lydia, her employer's wife, whom Edna had met once before, crossed the tall prairie grass, her dark hair gleaming in the prairie sun. She reached out and pulled Edna in for a hug. Willem wasn't far behind and tousled her hair. *Tousled it.* As though, at eighteen years of age, Edna were still a young child and not a woman grown. She might have been engaged had she not lied to Brandon about her departure day and snuck away.

Brandon. She'd promised herself she wouldn't think of him. Impossible to keep a promise like that. How could one control one's mind? Edna knew well that thoughts and emotions weren't something to be controlled, but endured.

One of the young men who drove the wagon unbuckled her trunk from the back of the coach and with large, helping hands he set it gingerly at her feet. A layer of dust from the road covered his clothes, a far cry from the Chicago men who had poured through the bakery's doors. Compared to Brandon, this man was positively unrefined, but the thought of such a difference showing itself so immediately after her arrival set her lips to smiling.

He didn't meet Edna's eyes. Rather, he turned to continue his labor when Lydia lifted a hand after him. "Hugh, when you're through unloading the guests' things, will you take Edna's trunk to Della's guest room?"

Her things taken care of, Edna turned her attention to the home before her. At first glance, it appeared modest, used as Edna was to the stacked, grand houses in Chicago. Della's home was like too-wet dough spreading its way out from the center. Its white clapboard sides and large windows were sure to house a young and happy family. What little she knew of Lydia's sister-in-law, Della, had told her the woman was practical and kind enough to house Edna for the fore-seeable future. Her eyes swept past the home and across what looked like miles of open land.

One look was all it took, and she understood why people risked everything to go west. Never had she felt as free as she did now. No bakery, no Brandon, no buildings towering over her, holding her down. Just a few squat structures. Modest, yes, but she could see the hills and trees between and beyond. Her sweeping gaze was like a sparrow cutting through the scene, free to soar high into the endless blue sky or dip low to graze the tips of the grass. No, this was nothing like Chicago. Her life here would be different. Here there was room to move, to breathe.

Lydia turned to Edna. "Willem is working on our house. We'll be out of the guest house soon, and you can move in there."

"Oh, the spare room will do nicely." Edna shook her head, hoping to convey that she didn't need any special accommodations. She wasn't here for the housing or even for the pay. While both of those were more than generous, Edna had moved west because her mother had practically forced her to take this position. Mama knew, as well as Edna did, that Edna would have never been able to quit Brandon. They were bound like salt and pepper. For better or worse.

The guests who had accompanied Edna on the journey hefted their own trunks from the ground near Edna's. Theirs were much smaller. They didn't need as much as Edna. They would only stay the week before heading back to their cushy homes in Chicago.

The man, Hugh, lifted her trunk again, and Lydia and Edna followed him into the sprawling rambler. The entry had a wood floor, smoothed by years of boots traversing its planks. As they rounded a wall, they entered the kitchen, but the room was more than that. It was an open space, and no visitor could avoid it. One way or another, they'd pass through. The oven was the center of this home, a trait she was well used to.

A bowl covered with a cloth sat on the counter, no doubt dough rising to be baked in the morning. The sight made her heart twinge. It would be a long while before she saw her mama again.

A young girl with light brown hair turned and tsked at Hugh's boots. "Hugh, I'll have to sweep."

"Sorry, sis. Couldn't take 'em off. My hands are full." He spoke over his shoulder and continued down the hall.

Lydia drew Edna into the kitchen. "Edna, this is Fay Morris. She works for Della."

Fay smiled, her head fell to one side, and her shoulders dipped as though a great load had been removed. "I'm grateful you're here. I had a dream you'd missed the train, and Lydia and I were left to manage the guests."

Lydia squeezed Edna's arm. "I'm glad you didn't miss the train."

Edna gave a tight smile. These women didn't realize how close she had been to *not* coming. It was only due to her mother's quick thinking that they avoided Brandon coming to the train station and convincing Edna to stay. Ma had told him Edna wouldn't leave for another two weeks. That they still needed to train her replacement in the bakery before Edna could go anywhere. Brandon's older sister had let slip that he was saving for a ring. That he'd planned to propose to keep her in town. They hadn't given him the chance.

Edna's throat grew thick. Wasn't that what every girl wanted, a man on his knee with a ring in his hand? That was what she'd wanted for so long. So why was she glad to be far from him? Why did she feel that she stood a bit taller, walked a bit lighter?

Hugh returned, his hands empty, and gave Edna a tight smile and a nod as he exited the house.

Edna turned to Fay. "Let me sweep. He couldn't take off his boots because his hands were full with my things."

Fay eyed Edna for a moment before passing her the broom with a smile. "Welcome to Aster Ridge."

Edna had barely begun running the broom along the wooden floor when Hugh returned. He strode right to Edna, and she froze at his unexpected attention.

"I don't mind cleaning up my own messes." He took the broom from her startled fingers, and though the object was small in his grip, he moved it with a deftness that told her he truly was used to cleaning up after himself.

This fact didn't fit with what little she knew of men. They commanded a room. They didn't sweep dirt from its corners.

At that thought, her mind conjured up the image she'd been trying her best not to imagine—Brandon reading her letter. The one where she apologized for leaving without saying goodbye, for lying to him about her departure date, and wishing he would find happiness without her.

Would he rage about, taking out his anger on those around him? Would he be sad when there was no Edna to glean comfort from? So many times she'd wondered how much of his emotion had been for show, to punish her for whatever he was cross with her about. She wasn't there now, and she never would be again. She drew a deep breath and tried to smile. Things would be different here. For the first time in her life, she could see who she was without Brandon's influence.

BY THE END of the week, Edna and Fay worked in tandem, making food for Della's household as well as Willem's guests. She hadn't expected such a companion and found she liked Fay's playful manner and hard work.

Edna had even ridden with Fay's family, the Morrises, into town for the Yuletide dance. Edna hadn't had much chance to view the town on her journey to Aster Ridge. She watched with greedy attention now. The storefronts were simple but clean, and townsfolk lined the sides as they made their way to the large building where the dance would be held.

Once they'd delivered their food to the buffet table, Fay tugged Edna close. "Now that we're done, let's make ourselves available. It's always a treat watching the men of Dragonfly Creek clamor over a newcomer."

Edna looked at her new friend sidelong. "You make it sound like I'm a piece of meat being fought over by a pack of dogs."

Fay only narrowed her eyes and gave Edna a wolfish smile. She took Edna's elbow and they stood on the side with their arms linked.

Edna surveyed the crowd. Willem's guests were the best-dressed, and after serving them three meals a day for a week, Edna could pick out each of them with ease. Most of the other men were locals identifiable not only because of their unfamiliar faces, but because they wore more casual attire.

Fay raised her hand to her mouth and covertly pointed at a family just arriving. "See the eldest one? That's Catherine Price. Hugh has been sweet on her for as long as I can remember. Just younger than her is Jeremy. He's strong as an ox and nearly as dumb, but he'll make a decent living. Their father is the blacksmith, and I guess grit is all he needs to take over the family business."

Then her face brightened at something behind Edna, and she reached out. "Hugh, show Edna how we do things here in Dragonfly Creek." Fay took her brother's forearm and pulled it toward Edna. He seemed larger here among this throng of folks, as though his stature was built for labor on a farm, not twirling a dancer. But his clothes were neat, and his light brown hair was combed, though it possessed a slight wave no amount of water would be able to tame indefinitely.

Fay tugged on his arm, but his body didn't move any closer, as though unwilling to let his sister control more than the lower half of his arm. It was no wonder. Fay had only just finished telling Edna Hugh had a sweetheart. His face was stoic, almost irritated, and Edna shifted at Fay's insistence.

Edna lifted her hand, palm toward Hugh, stopping his unwilling approach. "I don't... need..." She shook her head as she spoke. Even as she was attempting to rebuff him, her heart danced a jig of its own in her chest.

Hugh cut her off, if it could even be called that when she could barely get the words out. "I'd be pleased if you'd allow me the first dance."

Even fake, his smile stretched wide and bright. Surely, he had any number of girls begging for his dark eyes to grace them with his attention. The first dance should go to that blacksmith's daughter he was sweet on. But his hand remained outstretched, waiting for Edna to reply. It would be rude to refuse, regardless if it wasn't his wish.

"Thank you." She slid her hand into his palm. It was rough and warm. Nothing like Brandon's palm, which was strong, but smoother and not quite as large. Funny how she'd never thought of Brandon's hand size before, but put her hand in another man's and she'd be able to tell it wasn't Brandon even with a kerchief over her eyes.

The first chord sounded, and Hugh led her onto the dance floor.

Edna pressed his arm. "I'm sorry. I didn't think—"

Hugh faced her, his brown eyes meeting hers, stealing her thoughts and therefore her words. "You'll learn Fay can be pushy. We all try to quell her need to matchmake, but sometimes it cannot be avoided."

Avoided? The word cut at Edna's pride. But the music started in earnest, a fast-paced, playful melody. Just as Edna was second-guessing her desirability as a partner, Hugh twirled and moved her with such speed that when she returned to him, she was laughing. Did it really matter if Hugh was keen on her? She was starting a new adventure, possibly the first one in her life. Now was the time to find who she was without the bakery and without Brandon. She didn't need this man—or any of these men— to adore her.

They danced, him pushing her away only to pull her back

again, his rough palm catching on the cheap lace lining the waist of her dress. Try as she might, she couldn't ignore the touch of his hand or the heat that bled through her clothes and warmed her skin.

When the song ended, she was breathless with heat in her cheeks. He deposited Edna next to Fay's side once more and hurried away. Possibly to steer clear from Fay's *matchmaking*, as he'd called it, but still, the quickness of his retreat sliced. The feeling of being discarded hurt more than she'd like to admit. Was that how Brandon had felt when he'd read her goodbye note?

Her mother's words before she'd left rang in her ears. "You cannot replace your pa with a husband."

Was that what she'd been doing with Brandon? Putting up with poor treatment for the sake of being loved? She hadn't wanted to believe it.

She straightened her spine and threw back her shoulders. True or not, it was the past, and she was looking forward now. This was a new start. Though she might still be cursed with that want for love, she would control it. She would do her work, and if a man came courting, she would assess whether that man evoked emotions that could be controlled. If he made her heart beat faster or her cheeks flush, she would avoid him.

She'd already taken her first lesson.

Avoid Hugh Morris.

2

---

9 MONTHS **later**

EDNA ROUNDED the corner of the house to find the goat pen empty. The gate was wide open, and the wire used to keep it shut was missing, no doubt lost somewhere in the grass. She squeezed the handle to the milking bucket and, spinning, cast a glance east toward the mouth of the valley. The goats had gone home. This wasn't the first time.

She stopped by the barn and traded her bucket for a large roll of twine. Then she turned up her collar, readying for the long trek to the Morris household. The goats used to belong to them and had never gotten used to their new home.

She started off, quickly veering onto the worn path so she didn't ruin her skirts in the dewy morning grass. The cold wind was similar to the winds in Chicago, except there she'd only had to bear the chill as she moved from one building to another. Here, there was nothing for miles. No buildings to stop the gusts and, even on the Graham's homestead, the outbuildings were much further than one door down.

Edna recalled who, exactly, had lived one door down in Chicago. As cold as December might be, this way of life was better. Here, folks had to be intentional to court one another. Despite Fay's attempts, Edna had held firm in her wish to be without a man at her side. Or towering over her.

As she came around the bend, Fay appeared in the distance, walking alongside Hugh. Fay raised a hand in greeting, and Edna lifted her own in reply. No matter that she was walking in the cold to collect unruly goats, Edna couldn't help but smile at Fay's lightness, her carefree attitude. These past months Fay had become Edna's closest friend.

As they neared one another, Fay bore a mischievous smirk. "The goats?"

Edna nodded.

Fay cocked her head at her brother. "Perhaps we should start checking the pen before we leave in the morning. We could save Edna the trip."

Unwilling to chat in such a biting breeze, Edna moved past them and pivoted to walk backward. "We just need to find a way to keep the children from leaving the gate open."

Fay pressed Hugh's arm. "Go with Edna. You know Briar can put up a fight. Edna doesn't need to wrestle a goat this morning." She snorted. "Or any morning."

Edna greatly wanted his help, for Briar was aptly named, and more than once she'd wished the Grahams would ask her to make goat stew.

With a laugh, he broke away from Fay and joined Edna. "I'm only coming because I'd like to watch you wrestle a goat."

She laughed and nudged him with her elbow.

He found his footing once more and they walked together, him in the grass and her on the thin footpath that led between the houses.

His hands hid deep in his pockets, likely to keep the chill

away. He had a pair of work gloves tucked into his back pocket.

"Are gloves a fashion statement now?" she asked.

He gave her a quizzical look before touching the gloves with a smile. "Yes. I would think a Chicagoan like yourself would know a thing or two about what is stylish." He heaved a sigh. "I guess I'll just have to teach you."

She laughed, and her heart surged, almost touching the back of her throat. She clamped her lips shut. This teasing was awfully close to flirting, and Edna knew better. Not only was she avoiding men, but Hugh had a sweetheart. It was taking him time to pin her down, but one only had to see them together to know this easy banter, this way Hugh had of making Edna at ease, it wasn't only Edna who drew it out of him. It was Hugh. Kind, easy, gentle. Nobody would think Catherine Price a fool for waiting around for a man like him, no matter how long it had been.

She glanced at the horizon. The sunrise painted the sky a pale yellow, which would shortly blaze into a brilliant orange. "I understand why you got rid of Briar. He's a bully, and he leads the others astray."

Hugh's face stretched into a smile. "You just have to show him who's boss."

Edna laughed. "*He's* the boss! It's not as though I can throw him over my shoulder like a sack of flour."

Hugh looked at her with a doubtful cast to his brows. "You couldn't heft a sack of flour."

Edna scoffed and gave him a coy smile. "I can. My mother owns a bakery, don't you know."

Of course he knew. Everyone did. Her mother's reputation was the very reason she'd been hired to work the Grahams' gentlemen's ranch. Edna counted herself lucky that the Morrises didn't have any more daughters, otherwise she had no doubt another would have been hired in her stead. And Edna fairly shuddered to think where she would be today had she not been recruited for the ranch.

Hugh's cheek twitched into a half smile. "Is that so?"

"Yes."

They came upon the first goat, grazing at the gate of its old pen. Edna had half a mind to ask the Morrises if they could just keep the animals and let the Grahams continue paying for their feed. Only it was a sight easier to walk a goat across the valley on occasion than to try hauling a pail of milk every day.

Edna pulled the roll of twine from her apron pocket and looped it around the goat's neck. The remaining four goats grazed nearby, and she attached the rest to the twine and started for the ranch.

She glanced at the goats trailing her. "Briar isn't giving me any grief today. I'm sorry to have wasted your time."

Hugh lifted a shoulder and let it drop. "No more than Fay does anytime there's a new batch of guests. She thinks her hair looks different if she spends an extra quarter of an hour fixing it."

Edna laughed. "Does it not? That's discouraging to hear you men don't notice those things."

Hugh glanced at her, then away. Short. Dismissive. The same way he'd been at that first country dance. He'd never noticed her. She couldn't compete with Catherine, his childhood love. By now, Edna knew better than to try.

In the months since her arrival, they had fallen into a friendship bordering on siblinghood. Since the Morris children were all young and unmarried, Edna would often accompany them to the various activities the town or Willem's ranch would put on. She watched as women eyed Hugh, never going near him, either from fear of or respect for Catherine. Perhaps, if things had been different, Edna would have been horrified to be thought of as a near-sibling to a man as handsome as Hugh. But Edna didn't mind. She was a broken music box and her tune played off-key. Unlike most women, who were doing their darndest to nail a man down, Edna was avoiding them at all costs.

She liked to watch him, but her watching was innocent, pretend. The same way a girl feels while reading a dime-store romance. He wasn't hers to love, but she could still enjoy imagining what life with him would be like. He'd taught her that not every man was like Brandon. Not every man withheld his love until he needed forgiveness. Not every man yelled himself hoarse in a fit of jealous rage.

Some men cared for their families and those around them. Some men worked hard and still had a bit of happiness left at the end of a difficult day.

A simple friendship was exactly what she needed. Edna knew by now that she wasn't strong enough to break away once she loved someone. It was better to keep her mind distant, her eyes down and her hands in a batch of dough.

The thin twine jerked and slipped from her grip. Briar had apparently decided he'd behaved for long enough and was due a snack. He munched half-dead grass, though he had good feed at the Grahams, and the rest of the line stopped with him, following suit and touching their own lips to the stiff blades. Hugh took a few more steps before turning. Edna didn't want to beg his help, but she knew from experience there was no forcing Briar to move when he'd made up his mind.

Hugh shook his head and smirked as he plucked the twine from the grass next to Briar's head. "We notice plenty about you women. It's been my experience that it's never the things you wish for us to notice. It's not the well-groomed parts that are most interesting. It's the flaws, the outbursts, the mistakes. Everything else, well, it's too normal to be noticeable."

Edna snickered. "If you think that's flattery, you may want to stick to farming."

A slight frown tugged at his mouth before he bent to tug on Briar's horn. "C'mon, boy."

Edna winced at her careless words. Hugh had little choice in his profession. He merely farmed because their small plot of land was all they had to their name, and it was the only way to keep supper on the table. Watching him now, she could not deny he had a knack for animals. Briar trotted alongside Hugh's boots as though Hugh had promised a carrot at the end of the road. She should have complimented his abilities instead of making this seem like a last resort.

Edna reached a hand out for the twine rope. "I can hold that."

Hugh slanted his mouth in an almost smile. "I believe I can manage."

Edna huffed. If Hugh hadn't come back with her, she might have been forced to stay in this windswept valley, tugging Briar's horn until the early afternoon. "Why does he like you?"

Hugh kept his eyes forward. "Some say I'm a likable fellow."

Edna's hand twitched. She wanted to push at his arm in a playful way, the way Fay did. But close as she might be to their family, Edna was no sibling, and that reflex was likely to muddle the line between friendship and affection. That line was a dangerous one to walk. She had grown close in friendship with Brandon, and eventually Brandon had taken that friendship to mean he had a claim on her.

The laugh died in her throat, and she turned away from Hugh. A mere nine months since she'd left Chicago, and she was already losing her memories, her resolve. She'd not come here to catch a man—that was Fay's goal. Edna was here to eke out a living, to be happy without Brandon's influence, to learn who she was outside of the shadow of her mother's booming bakery. If a man did come along, she would have to be the picture of logic. Emotions had ensnared her before, but never again. When the time came, she would choose a man who elicited few emotions, one who was gentle and good.

Hugh cleared his throat. "Are you headed to Chicago for Christmas?"

Heavens no, but she couldn't tell him that. As far as anyone knew, Willem Graham had offered her too much money to refuse. They believe she left Chicago for no other reason than to work for his ranch here in Montana.

"Not this year," she said. "The travel is too extensive, and I don't want to be a bother to anyone." Travel here was much different than in the city. Women out west rarely went far from home without a man, and most of the females in this valley carried a pistol in their apron pocket.

Hugh gave her a puzzled look. "A bother? Nobody would mind helping you to get home for Christmas. You should be with your mother."

A lump rose in Edna's throat. There was little she would like better than to spend Christmas in their apartment above the bakery. She could almost feel the fire warming her toes. Her mother would be next to her, resting her swollen feet on the mantle and drinking a touch of watered brandy. "Maybe next year."

Hugh fell silent, and Edna was glad he wasn't the type to push the subject. Fay would have talked circles around Edna, inventing ways Edna could go to the moon if that was what she wanted. Not even Fay knew that the desire to go home was as dangerous as being there. Nine months wasn't long enough for her to forget about Brandon. No amount of time could cut him from her mind. He was forever entwined in her childhood memories, casting darkness on what should have been carefree, innocent days.

Her mother had known enough by the end. That was why she'd insisted on Edna taking the position with Willem. The money, though generous, had hardly mattered. It was possible Edna's mother would rather see her indentured to Willem than married to Brandon. It was a fact she'd be hard pressed to explain to a stranger, how a servant could be freer than a wife. And yet she knew it with bone-deep surety.

3

ONCE THEY REACHED THE RANCH, Hugh passed the twine to Edna. Their fingers brushed, and he wished he'd worn his gloves so he wouldn't have had to feel her cold fingers against his own. He moved away from her, leaving her to the goats and heading to the stables where he would find plenty of hard work to take his mind off her. He'd never told Fay he admired Edna, but somehow his sister knew.

He wanted to curse Fay for her meddling. He'd have stayed back to help Edna on his own, but Fay pressing him into it altered the innocence of such an offer. It was unfair how she took pleasure in forcing he and Edna together. Fay was intent on marrying rich, richer than anyone in their small town. Yet her hypocrisy showed when she expected Hugh to be blind to the fact that Edna had plenty of options. Those men might not be rich enough for Fay, but all were far better than him.

Hugh was a good enough man, but Edna deserved someone with a future. She was smart and plucky...she would do things in this life. She would have to be a fool to throw her purse in with a man like him. Poor, rough, and without a future.

Hugh entered the stable and fell into the usual pattern of morning tasks. He fed and watered the animals, opened the gate, and shooed the cows out into the cold to graze on whatever grass remained. Only, today these chores no longer occupied his mind. He knew them too well, like how his mama could knit without looking at her hands and still command the household.

He couldn't stop thinking of Edna and how she should be home with her family for Christmas. The Grahams were a good family, and their Christmas would be everything the holiday should be. Except it wouldn't have Edna's mother. Maybe he could talk to Willem, do something to get Edna's mother out here for Christmas.

Bastien, Willem's brother and the ranch owner, had hired two new hands in addition to Hugh, and when they took their break for lunch, Hugh made the cold trek up the south hill to Willem's homestead. The house was finished, but the barn was newly started. The corner posts had been set and the frame was nearly as tall as Willem. Hugh smiled to think the outbuilding might be complete by the end of the year.

Willem tipped his hat in greeting and set his tools down.

Hugh ran his gaze over the stable's exterior. "It's coming along."

Willem came to Hugh's side and turned so he was looking up at the structure from the same perspective. "So long as the weather behaves. Did you come to help?"

Hugh laughed. "I might be able to sneak over later."

Willem grinned in his easy way and slapped Hugh on the back. "I was only teasing. You've got enough work between your farm and Bastien's." Willem leveled Hugh with a look. "How is Lachlan doing?"

Hugh shrugged at the mention of his brother, who was

still learning how to live with malaria. "He's well. He's intent upon lengthening the time between treatments. Mother is incensed that she can't force him into following doctor's orders."

Willem nodded and started for the opening where the barn doors would eventually be hung. "I will need a bit of help when I lay the trusses."

Hugh followed Willem into the barn, glancing up at the open area soon to be covered in timber and shingles. "I'd be happy to help."

Willem drank from a water skin and offered it to Hugh. "What brings you to our hill?"

Hugh accepted the skin but didn't drink. Instead, he worked the cork into the opening and twisted at it. "D'you think we could bring Edna's mother out here for Christmas?"

Willem's brows twitched, and Hugh got the familiar impression that Willem always knew too much. He was an expert at reading faces, almost at reading minds.

"Doubtful," Willem said. "This is a busy time of year for the bakery. I figured Edna would be going home." He frowned. "Now that you mention it, she hasn't said anything yet. It's getting close to Christmas."

Hugh shook his head, remembering Edna's pursed lips, her nose pink with cold. A tendril of her amber hair falling across her cheek. "She said she feels like a nuisance asking for travel help. I'd be willing to take her to Billings at no cost." Hugh and Lachlan were the Grahams' hired drivers, taking the coach to Billings and back when they had guests to transport.

Willem scratched at his chin. "She should know better than to think herself a nuisance. You're welcome to take the coach if she decides she wants to have Christmas in Chicago."

Hugh passed the water skin back to Willem. "I'll let her know."

It was a simple phrase, and yet something bloomed in his belly. She was going to see her mama after nine months at Aster Ridge. Edna was getting the chance to go home. He grinned at the image, though admittedly, when he pictured Edna in a sitting room that wasn't the Grahams, he pictured her in his own, surrounded by his family.

If only.

Edna sat for dinner, her role being somewhere between a family member and a servant. She worked for Willem's gentlemen's ranch, but when they didn't have guests, she worked alongside the women in the family, contributing to the running the homestead.

After grace was said, dishes were passed around until plates were piled high with buttered beans, potatoes smothered in gravy, and Della's flaky biscuits.

Willem cleared his throat and everyone's attention fell on him. "Edna, I'm not sure what you have planned for the holidays, but I've sent a wire to the train station in Billings. They have a ticket to Chicago waiting for you, and Hugh has volunteered to transport you to Billings and back."

Edna's throat shriveled like one of those plums they'd laid out to dry in the sun over the summer. "Thank you." What else was there to say? *No, thanks. I'd rather never see that city again.* Or *if I go, I may never come back.* This was all sounding too dreary. It wasn't as though her life was at risk in Chicago. Only her *living* was at risk. She'd never been able to quit Brandon. He was like a burr deep in the sole of a shoe, forced so deeply into the leather that removing it now was impossible. She'd had to leave the sole behind and hope her feet could stand being bare. "Mother will be so pleased to have me."

Not true. Her mother would assume Edna's return meant she was done at Aster Ridge. That she was fired, for what other cause could Edna have for returning so soon? Brandon would assume the same. Would it be possible to stay out of Brandon's notice? Would he even care? Surely, with Edna gone, another woman had filled her place in his life. Perhaps he was even married by now, but that wishful thought was fleeting. While her mama's letters might be bare of any mention of Brandon, she knew for certain her mama would be all too pleased to announce Brandon's marriage to anyone besides her own daughter.

The meal continued, and Edna prayed she hid the turmoil swirling inside. Her mother might not be pleased at her imminent visit. But was she never to see her mother again? Brandon claimed he loved her, so would he truly wish to run her off entirely? Perhaps the strength she'd gained these nine months meant when she left this time, she could do it openly, without fear he would come to the station and try to convince her to marry him. But what if seeing him made her as weak as she'd been the day she left? The thought made her pull her hands off the table and twist them in her lap.

She hated being so easily swayed by him. He wasn't everything to her. He was right when he said nobody would love her like he did, but that didn't mean nobody would *ever* love her. His love was unique because he'd been like a brother to her growing up, and had helped more than once when a bakery customer had the poor sense to linger in hopes of winning affection from Edna.

The problem was, Edna knew him too well. Brandon wasn't all bad. He was hard, but that was because his father was the same. Edna figured she was a lot like her mother. That was the nature of life. Young men and women reflect that which they see. A girl sees a strong woman making her way in a bustling city, and she learns to do the same. If a boy sees his father ruling his home with a heavy hand and a gruff voice, he'll treat others the same.

Only Brandon had a touch of his mother, too. She was the gentlest person Edna had ever met. Edna had often wondered how Brandon's parents found one another. From the outside, they looked to be opposites, but perhaps that was exactly why they were together. Mr. Clareview wouldn't have wanted a strong woman like Mama. He wanted to rule his household, and sure enough, he did.

If Brandon favored his father, did that mean Edna was less like her mama and more like Mrs. Clareview? She didn't like to think so, didn't want to imagine herself with that beaten-down appearance. Her heart ached for Mrs. Clareview and the way life had turned out for her. She also feared for Brandon's younger siblings, especially the girls. They loved their pa, and why would they hold out, waiting for a man who was any better? Luck would have to be on their side. Not everyone had a wealthy benefactor who could whisk them away to live in rugged Montana.

ON SATURDAY, Edna forgot her cares in the hum of activity preceding the town's Christmas dance. She smirked at Fay, who worked alongside her in the kitchen preparing pies and pastries to contribute on behalf of both the Graham and Morris families.

"Anyone you're hoping to see tonight?" Edna asked.

Fay tossed Edna a coy smile. "Not unless one of them has received an inheritance I don't know about."

There had been a time when Edna wanted to chide her friend for her shallowness, but she'd seen what Fay's family situation had done to her, to all of the Morris children. All who remained felt trapped at their parents' side. Edna had heard talk in town about how Hugh caught the eye of every new girl, only to fall out of favor once that girl realized she, too, would be saddled with his crippled father and the family's over-mortgaged farm.

And now Lachlan, plagued with malaria. It wasn't an uncommon sickness, but it was another weight for the Morrises to carry. Edna had written to an old friend, an apothecary in Chicago named Frederick. Having not received a reply, she wondered...did Frederick remember Brandon's snarls? Remember Brandon's fist in Frederick's gut when all he'd done was hold Edna's arm as she crossed the cobbled street? Edna remembered it all with far too much clarity. She understood if Frederick wasn't keen to experience another of Brandon's displays of authority, if he never spoke to her again, even when Edna now lived hundreds of miles away.

Edna leaned over and bumped Fay with her arm. "You know, my mama made it without a man. You don't need to marry rich to be comfortable." How could she convince Fay that what had happened to Mr. Morris was the exception and not the rule?

Fay stared hard at the dough she was folding. "I'm *comfortable* enough. I want more. I want my children to be educated. I want bacon on Christmas morning, and a toy for each sock" — Fay slid her eyes toward Edna—"a toy that isn't homemade."

"There's a reason those things are your standard for normal. It's the way most of the families in this town live. You could have that life with several of the men in town."

Fay lifted her chin. "None of them went to university."

"University isn't everything. Oft times a man can do better at a trade than whatever he'll do with his education. I know lawyers who aren't as well-off as the cobbler next door."

Edna bit her lip at her use of Brandon's trade. Why had she mentioned him? Ever since her walk with Hugh the other morning, she'd found it difficult to put Brandon in the back of her mind where he belonged.

Fay twisted her mouth in the way she did when she was considering. "Christian was a veterinarian, and I think he did just fine before the inheritance, but he went to school for that trade."

Mel and Christian were newly married and had recently bought a large portion of the Morris' farm, joining in this patchwork family that settled this wide valley.

Edna shrugged. "Sometimes a bit of school is required. What is important is that he loves what he does. Everything else, well, most of the time, it falls into place."

Fay gave Edna a curious glance. "You make it sound like a man can choose his profession."

Edna laughed. "And why can't he?"

"Well." Fay seemed to choke on her words. "He does what his father does, or whatever is available when he's old enough to find an apprenticeship."

Edna nodded. "True. But there are some men who are blessed with the temperament to be content wherever they go. Those are the ones you want to look for. They will make your home a happy place, and not somewhere he comes when he's wrung out from the day."

Edna didn't know where this was all coming from. She'd not thought much about a husband since coming to Aster Ridge. She'd not thought much about the qualities of a husband *before* she'd come. Who was she to be spouting tips on men and marriage when she'd lived most of her life with a father in the ground and only a bakery to replace the loss?

4

EDNA TOOK one last peek in the looking glass before she exited her room. Another dance. Another chance to see how far she was from entertaining a suitor. She could dance and smile, but she had yet to let Bastien know she was allowing visitors. She still lived in Bastien and Della's home, though Willem and Lydia had since moved into their recently finished home on the south end of the valley. Della had offered the guesthouse, but Edna was fine in her small room. She tried not to acknowledge how lonely she'd be out in that guest house all alone.

Constant companionship was one of the benefits of living in this valley. In Chicago, it had only been her mama, and most of the time one of them was working in the bakery. It was nice to be in a home with people around all the time.

Perhaps when Fay was ready to be on her own, the two of them could find a place together. Edna smiled at the thought. She would be anything but bored if Fay was her housemate. Fay had high hopes for a husband, and she was clever enough to get exactly what she wanted. Edna just hoped she kept in mind the practical dreams and not just the idealistic ones.

Edna joined the rest of the household in the kitchen. Della was tying matching purple ribbons in Violet's hair while Joshua sucked happily on his thumb. Edna scooped him into her arms and nuzzled his neck. Violet was a darling and bound to grow into a beauty to rival her mother, but Joshua had Edna's heart. More than once, Edna had been tending the children and the wish had come upon her that these were her children and not another's.

Della smiled at Edna. "You look lovely."

Edna moved Joshua to her hip and smoothed her skirt with her free hand. One look told her her Sunday best were rags compared to what Della wore. Della's dress had been bought in Chicago—Edna could almost guess the shop with its hooked-nose dressmaker. A pang of longing struck her, and she looked away from the reminder. She didn't miss the city so much as she missed her mama.

Bastien came inside and blew into his hands. "I'm ready when you are. It's as cold as a mountain in Wyoming tonight. Are you sure you want to go?"

Della leveled Bastien with a stare. "Wyoming mountains don't frighten me."

He laughed and tucked his wife under his arm, whispering something in her ear.

Edna turned away from the scene and lifted Joshua's blanket from where he'd been sitting. She wrapped it around him and followed the rest of the Grahams out the front door.

Violet took Edna's free hand, and Edna allowed herself one last look at the couple in front of her and tried not to be jealous of the kindness they showed one another. Brandon never would have been that way to her. It was good she'd come, but what of going back? Had she grown strong enough these last several months that she would be able to resist him?

Once they reached the wagon, Edna tucked herself in the

bed with the children. Willem and Lydia came out with their children and joined her in the back. By the time everyone was settled, Edna found she was quite warm. All except her cheeks and nose, which would be quite rosy by the time they arrived.

And rosy they were. Unfortunately, she'd also gained a sniffle, one she hoped she could keep quiet for the sake of her partners. Fay appeared, tugging Hugh behind her as though she needed his companionship. He bobbed his acknowledgement to Edna, then cast a look over the grange hall. Probably looking for Catherine Price.

Edna ignored the pluck in her chest at the thought of Hugh dismissing her so quickly in Catherine's favor. It wasn't the first time, nor would it be the last. Edna wasn't looking for romance anyway. She'd started too young and now it was time to set romance on the windowsill to cool for a bit. She would enjoy her work and herself. For she'd found the time in Aster Ridge had brought out a spirited attitude she'd never had the courage to show outside her mother's kitchen.

When the first chord struck, Fay released her hold on Hugh. "I'm going to see who needs a partner." She pushed at Hugh's back, causing him to sway toward Edna as Fay hustled away from the two.

Edna had the feeling Fay had planned this and had been holding tight to Hugh for just this purpose.

Hugh cocked his head. "Would you dance with me, Edna Archer?"

Edna laughed at this all too familiar circumstance. She took his outstretched hand. She'd be lying if she said there was no spark between her and Hugh. What she didn't know was whether he felt it too. Perhaps his mind was on Catherine, or perhaps he preferred brunettes over Edna's red hair.

Hugh cleared his throat and, rather than meet his eyes,

she stared at a patch of stubble that peppered his Adam's apple. He must have missed it when he'd shaved for the dance.

His fingers tightened on her waist, guiding her through the dance. "Willem says you're planning on going to Billings."

It was Edna's turn to clear her throat and, to her embarrassment, sniff her running nose. "Yes."

"He's given me leave to take you in the coach. When would you like to go?" With a gentle hand, he pressed her into a spin.

Edna had been putting this conversation off, hoping if she waited long enough, some farm emergency would occur and they wouldn't be able to spare Hugh or herself. But Christmas was just over a week away. If she waited much longer, they would both be traveling on Christmas Eve.

She came back, placing her hand on his shoulder once more. "I suppose whenever you can find the time." Without guests to attend, her presence wasn't needed by any of the Grahams.

They swayed to the music and Edna's movements became less sure, more limp.

Hugh's hand tightened on her waist, an involuntary jerk. "Monday should be fine. We best go sooner rather than later. Lachlan is overdue for a spell, and I'm not keen to drive alone."

Sometimes she forgot how lawless this place was. Hugh and Lachlan drove the coach together, with rifles close at hand. It wasn't like traveling in Chicago, where one might be pickpocketed by a small, starving child. Here, there was still word of lawless Indians and bands of outlaws looking to take everything, down to the pin from a lapel.

"Monday then." The song ended and Hugh removed his hands, leaving a chill behind even as he escorted her off the dance floor. She was truly going to Chicago. There wasn't any time to write to her mother. It would have to be a surprise. A Christmas miracle, or a disappointment. Either way, it was happening.

A flash of color caught Edna's eye—Catherine Price in a teal dress that set off the color of her curls.

Edna glanced at Hugh, risking her heart in the process. He was everything she wanted in a man, and she knew the moment he released her, he would go to Catherine. Desperate to keep him close for one moment more, her mind circling on surprising her mama for Christmas, Edna had a thought. "Could I buy a fur from you? I want to make my mother a muff for Christmas."

He grinned at her, his eyes sparking as though he'd just been given a gift. "I have just the one."

Hugh deposited Edna at Fay's side and disappeared into the throng of folks waiting for the next song. Edna sighed after him, partially glad for his apathy toward her. Her mother would roll her eyes at Edna's longing, but her mother hadn't lived without a father. There was something most compelling about being loved by a man. Without a father to do the job, she had gobbled up Brandon's willingness to do it. It was a difficult habit to break, but so far she'd at least been able to keep the need to herself. Hugh didn't need to know how she longed for his attention, his teasing, or his assistance with any menial chore.

Fay nudged Edna. "Who are *they*? Both of them are as tall as ponderosas."

Edna followed Fay's gaze and spotted the gentleman newcomers. They approached Della and Bastien. One of them embraced Della and kissed her on the cheek.

A breath exploded like a curse from Fay. She spoke through clenched teeth. "It's Garrick Hampton. The weasel."

"Della's brother?" Edna surveyed the pair and figured the one who had his arms around Della must be her brother.

"And the reason my sister had to move to Oregon."

"I thought they moved because Eloise's husband was wanted."

Fay glared at the dancers, apparently refusing to look in Garrick's direction. "Well, yes, but he was successfully hiding out in Aster Ridge until Garrick turned him in. What is he even doing here? He's supposed to be on a boat somewhere, fighting Spaniards."

Garrick looked to be introducing his companion to his sister and brother-in-law. Then the men turned and stood shoulder to shoulder, surveying the dance floor. Garrick's eyes landed on Fay, and squinted. Edna glanced at her friend, whose eyes were glued to the dancers and her mouth was pursed with the effort of holding onto her hatred for Garrick.

Garrick broke away from his friend's side, striding toward Edna and Fay with a purposeful tilt to his brow.

Edna leaned toward her friend. "He's coming over."

Fay broke away and Edna stalled, undecided as to whether she should follow Fay and make their retreat a rebuff or stay put. Garrick reached her, his long legs spanning the distance in a blink. Just then a fiddle started up again, and the rest of the band joined.

Garrick stopped, his mouth working as he looked after Fay. Then he focused on Edna. "May I have this dance?"

Edna drew a deep breath to decline his offer, but manners and curiosity got the better of her. She accepted his outstretched hand. "Of course."

He led her onto the floor and they took a few turns before he spoke. "Your companion. Is she Fay Morris?" He jerked his head in the direction Fay had fled.

"Yes."

"It's only been three years, but she has turned into a woman." Admiration laced his voice.

If only this man knew Fay's feelings toward him. Edna had no doubt Fay would let him know as soon as she had the stomach to stand his company. Edna considered warning him, but there was no way to do so without being offensive, so she changed the topic. "I work for your sister and the Grahams." She didn't exactly work for Della, but it was the only connection she had with this stranger.

"Oh!" His smile brightened. "You must be Edna."

Edna laughed, shocked he would know of her. Her surprise must have shown on her face because Garrick smiled. "I missed home a great deal when I was away. I begged Della to write me long letters full of everything, even the mundane." He gave her that same curious look he'd given Fay from across the dance floor. "But you don't work for Della. You're Willem's girl."

Edna shifted under the title which could appear scandalous to the gossips in this small town. "I work for Willem, yes. And I help your sister whenever there are no guests."

"You took Eloise's position."

He made her sound like some thief. "*Filled*. I didn't have to take it, for she was already gone." Edna searched Garrick's face for guilt, but found none. "Are you home for Christmas?"

"The war is long over. We've been visiting families along the way. My friend Stimps here will head down to his family in Texas."

"He's going to miss Christmas with his family?" For even if he left tonight, Garrick's friend wouldn't make it to Texas in time for Christmas.

Garrick shrugged, and the song ended. He led her off the floor and over to his sister.

Della beamed at Garrick, then glanced at Edna. "I see you met my brother."

Edna smiled. "He's a fine dancer."

Garrick touched her elbow and said, "This here is Stimps. The best comrade I could have asked for."

Stimps cocked an eyebrow at Garrick. "Your friend here saved my life. I wanted to be sure to meet his family on my way home." He gave Della a small smile. Edna had to stop herself from staring at the bright pink scar that marred his cheek and ended at a curled ear. He faced Edna and stuck out a hand. "*Walter* Stimps. Hampton here can't seem to get my name right when introducing me to the rest of the world."

Edna took his outstretched hand, and they shook once before releasing their hold. "Garrick says you're from Texas?"

"Yes, ma'am. If you're ever down south, my mama would be thrilled to host a pretty young lady like yourself."

Edna blushed and moved closer to Della. "Where are the children?"

Della pointed to a bench along the wall. Joshua lay there, bundled and asleep. "Violet must be running around with Bridget somewhere." Della stretched her neck to look around the room, but her face was still smooth and unworried. There might be bandits on the road, but the towns themselves were quite safe. Children ran everywhere without fear of being trampled by a carriage. Edna's own childhood had been spent in her mother's bakery, not running around with the neighborhood children, and as soon as she could hold a rag she'd been set to work. Mama hated a dirty kitchen.

As much as she feared returning, part of her heart longed to go so badly, to smell the bakery in the morning when everything was done and the guests hadn't yet arrived. To be teased by her older customers who swore they had a grandson who was sure to be smitten with Edna as soon as he saw her. Edna had learned long ago that many of the upper crust in Chicago wouldn't arrange a match with Edna. It was the young ones who were starting to let those expectations fall away and marry for love, or for lust. Who knew, really. Either way, the two were bound together, and she hoped their marriages worked out, if not for their happiness, for the ability to disappoint the stiff aristocracy that still existed.

Would Edna want to be back there forever? Would she want to take over her mother's bakery when the time came? Or would she rather carve out a life among these hills and pines? To find herself a husband and raise a family among dirt roads rather than cobbled streets?

Again, the image of Hugh flashed in her mind. She tried to picture Walter's face. Scarred though he was, he was still quite handsome and had a light about him that she'd not expected from a man so recently come from a war. But no, Walter's handsome face would not do. It didn't cause her stomach to lift and press against her ribs, or her cheeks to fill with color.

Perhaps she couldn't shake Hugh's face from her mind because he was familiar. Perhaps that was the type of man she preferred. Brandon had been familiar, too. Nearly part of the family until she became a woman and everything changed.

Now she had this wonderful circle of friends here in Aster Ridge, all whom she had gained in the last nine months and without Brandon to protect her, she had still flourished. It was now apparent that his protection was not of her, but of himself.

Hugh twirled in front of her, Catherine Price in his arms. Edna's heart sank. What did her feelings for that man matter? He hoped to gain favor with another girl, a girl who he'd been sweet on since his own childhood. She watched them dance. How did Hugh handle watching other men pursue Catherine? How would he feel watching her laugh with another man? Would he be angry? Would he pound his fist into the wall? Would he escort Catherine home, just to hiss harsh words the entire distance?

But as she watched skirts swirl on the dance floor, her heart told her Hugh was a different sort. He would never do those things. He wasn't just better, he was a flight of stairs above Brandon. And he loved Catherine.

5

HUGH LET out a sigh and it settled dark and quiet around his brother and sister, as tired from the night's excitement as he. Fay rode next to him on the seat, glaring at the dark ground where the horses stepped. Lachlan lay in the back, overtired, a sure sign that a spell was near. Hugh let out a slow breath, thinking of Catherine Price. She tore him in two.

He enjoyed her company, that was sure as rain. But he'd watched his closest friend, Jimmy, marry a woman who wanted too much. Jimmy worked himself into an early grave trying to make his wife happy. Hugh knew in his gut that a life with Catherine would be much the same. And he was worse off than even Jimmy had been. At least Jimmy had had only his wife to care for. Hugh would still be tied to his family's welfare, and Catherine's family had not been kind to Hugh's. It seemed inevitable that if he married Catherine, he would be forced to turn away from his family eventually. So he kept her at arm's length, always a friend but nothing more. She claimed his smile, his mind even, but she hadn't yet stolen his heart.

He glanced over at Fay. "Is Garrick back for good, or just Christmas?"

Her eyes flashed, catching the moonlight. "How would I know? I avoided him."

Hugh angled his head so Fay wouldn't see the smile stretch across his face. "Will you feign sickness come Monday morning?"

Fay didn't answer, and Lachlan leaned over the side and was sick. Hugh slowed their horse, Lady, but by the time the wagon stopped, Lachlan had finished.

He wiped his mouth with his sleeve. "I guess it finally came."

Fay turned so her knees pressed against Hugh's legs. She gripped the back of the bench. "You should have taken the medicine. Then you wouldn't have had a spell."

Hugh blinked hard at her haughty attitude.

Lachlan shifted so his head rested on the side of the wagon. "I got an extra month by waiting. We need the money more than we need my labor. Hugh and you do all the work for our family anyway."

Fay met Hugh's eyes. The family had so far kept the secret that their sister, Eloise, had married a bandit to pay for Lachlan's medicine. Their mother had a small store of gold set aside for just that purpose. What Lachlan *had* discovered was the cost of his medicine and the need to have an apothecary to mix it. He had fixated on the price without realizing their family wasn't worse off for the purchase of it.

Hugh called for Lady to continue, then turned to his brother. "It's not only your work we need. We want you to be happy."

Lachlan gave a rueful shake of his head. "My life won't be like Pa's, but it will never be the same."

Hugh wasn't the only one who'd lived most of his life

sweet on the same girl. Over the last year, Lachlan had watched another man court and marry his own sweetheart.

Fay harrumphed. "Jenny Carver was entertaining Alexander long before you got sick. She was never going to marry you."

Hugh winced. Fay had never been a gentle sister. She'd always been too blunt for comfort. He urged the horse onward again and turned the conversation to Fay. "And what of you, dear sister? Any men to your liking tonight?"

"I wouldn't know. I spent most of the evening avoiding a certain someone."

"You were the only one." Even Catherine had danced with Garrick. He would be a fine catch for any woman in Dragonfly Creek. He might not be wealthy, but he was related to the Grahams, the richest family Hugh knew, and would no doubt have the seed money to start any venture he wanted and do it well.

Fay cocked her head at Hugh. "Catherine is allowed to dance with whoever she wants. I have it on good authority that she's still waiting on a word from you—or maybe four words."

Hugh shifted on the hard bench, unwilling to count out the words to any phrase she might mean. "She'll be waiting a long time."

"Hugh! Don't say that. You love Catherine."

Hugh didn't argue, just shook his head. That was just it. He didn't love her. And he was beginning to think he never would.

When they arrived at the house, Fay helped Lachlan inside, and Hugh put the wagon and Lady into the barn with a bit of feed and water. He stroked the horse's mane and pulled a shriveled apple from his pocket. "Sorry, girl. Just trust me. It's about as good as we're getting inside."

He closed the barn door and went inside. Pa was in his chair, and Ma had a bit of sewing in her lap.

She turned at the sound of the door. "How was the dance, darling?"

"Good."

Pa spoke, his voice scratchy from his cold. "Fay said Catherine had your arm most of the time."

He removed his hat and set it on the hook. "She did." He walked near and warmed his hands at the fire. Fay wouldn't mind telling them how Catherine wanted Hugh, but his sister's brutal honesty stopped when it came to telling their parents exactly why Hugh wouldn't marry the Price girl, or any other. He'd watched the hurt that had come over their mama when their sister Eloise refused to marry for the sake of the family. He imagined no mother would like to see a child put life on hold for their parents' sake.

Pa continued. "They're a good family, you know."

Hugh nodded. They were decent, like most families in town. Only the Prices tended to show their wealth a bit more. There was also that trouble between Catherine's younger sister and Fay, but perhaps Pa hadn't heard about that.

Pa coughed and Hugh turned, patting his pa's shoulder. "Let's get you into bed or you're never going to kick that cough."

Pa nodded and raised his arms to his son. Hugh lifted his pa, his legs hanging weightless, as they had for over a decade. He set him in bed and helped to arrange the blankets over his legs. Once they were past his waist, Pa could manage the rest. Hugh sat at the foot of the bed.

"Lachlan's down again. Might be for a week. We were supposed to drive the coach and team to Billings so Edna could be home for Christmas."

Pa nodded. "You'll have to go. Hope everyone is spending time with family and not on the road lookin' for trouble."

"Things will fall behind here." There was always something to do, even now that they'd sold the majority of their ranch to Mel and Christian Milnes.

"We'll do fine. Get that girl to her family."

Pa didn't say it, but the unacknowledged plea was there. *Earn the money for transporting.* Though Hugh had offered to drive Edna for free, Willem insisted that as his employee, it was Willem's duty to pay for her secure transport. The pay was better than anything else Hugh could earn. Most anyone could be a ranch hand, but not everyone could drive the six-team coach needed to transport Willem's guests to and from Billings. Not even Hugh should be doing it without someone riding shotgun. This was still a lawless country. But Lachlan wouldn't be able to ride with Hugh, not this time.

"We need to tell Lachlan about the money. We don't need to tell him about Eloise's part. He knows she's happy. Just tell him Aaron sent it because they're doing so well out there."

Pa released a deep sigh. "He doesn't feel like we need him. Feels like he's too weak to be of any use."

Hugh closed his eyes and settled his irritation. They needed Lachlan, just as they'd always needed him. But selling a portion of the ranch had beaten his brother down. It had done that to all of them, for it forced them to admit they would never get on the upside of their mortgage. Hugh had to work as a hired hand or they'd never survive. Same for Fay. They all had a part to play for this family.

"Talk to him." Hugh gripped his pa's toes through the blanket, though he knew he wouldn't feel the pressure. He saw the touch, and that was enough.

Pa nodded, then slipped into a coughing fit.

Mama bustled in with a cup in her hands. "Drink a bit of this before bed." She turned to Hugh. "Good night, son."

Hugh took his cue to leave them alone, hoping his pa would see the sense in encouraging Lachlan. His brother wasn't useless, and Lachlan's refusal to take his medicine might still lose them the opportunity to drive Edna to Billings. They needed the money and Hugh was willing to take the risk of riding through the state with a lone driver. That didn't mean Willem would agree. After all, it was his coach and horses at risk.

6

MONDAY CAME TOO SOON AND, unfortunately, without any emergencies to prevent Edna from leaving. Edna joined Fay in the kitchen, hoping to forget the carpet bag sitting on her bed, waiting to be taken with her to Chicago. She glanced at Fay and noticed a scowl on her face.

"Bad morning?" Edna tried. Garrick and his friend had ridden home from the dance on Saturday alongside the Grahams' wagon and were asleep in the bunkhouse now. Edna wondered how Fay felt, knowing she was working harder to make extra food for a man she despised.

Fay passed a hand over her hair and ran it down her braid. "Lachlan's had a spell. He's not doing well this morning."

To Edna's shame, her heart lifted in her chest like a deer listening for danger. Only, instead of danger, this might be the emergency Edna had been waiting for. She went to Fay's side and asked, "Does he need to head into town for his treatment?" She admittedly knew little about his disease, or the treatment, when she'd begged Frederick's help. Not that she'd received a reply from him.

Fay shook her head. "We have the medicine. But he was so sick." Fay finally met Edna's gaze. "I don't know how he'll live this way. An entire life waiting for the next spell. In pain when it comes, but anxious over its arrival when it's not there." Her eyes shimmered with unshed tears. "Just when the rest of us are finding ways to live our own lives, his life has to be…this."

The sound of the front door opening broke the spell. Fay sniffed and blinked away the shine that had gathered in her eyes.

Willem came around the corner and greeted them. He took a fork and began eating potatoes from the pan, glancing at Edna. "I think Hugh is nearly ready for you."

Edna took a step backward. "I—isn't…" She looked at Fay.

Fay's brows drew together and she took Edna by her shoulders. "I'm sorry. You must have been listening to me and fearing your holiday was to be canceled."

Willem spoke through the food in his mouth. "*I* won't be the reason your mother is missing you on Christmas morning."

"But Hugh won't have a companion," Edna tried, the situation slipping through her fingers like a bar of soap in a washtub.

Willem waved her away. "It's too cold for an ambush. Anyway, Hugh is keen with a rifle." Then, as though he wasn't ruining Edna's morning, and her Christmas, and possibly a long time after, he turned to Fay. "Walter and Garrick are planning to stay through Christmas. With Edna being gone, can you assist taking the load off Lydia and Della?"

Edna stepped closer. "I can stay. You've guests and it is *my* job."

Willem laughed. "Not at all. He's not a paying customer. He's family. I only…" He glanced behind him and leaned closer to the women. "Well, Lydia needs a bit of extra help these days."

Edna's heart twitched. "A new baby?"

Willem nodded vigorously. No matter that her attempts to stay here were being thwarted time and time again, she couldn't help the smile that spread. Willem had been her family's benefactor for as long as she could remember. He was like some distant, wealthy cousin, and the thought of him having a child was as close to a niece or nephew as Edna was ever going to get.

"Congratulations." Edna offered him a warm smile.

He straightened and cast a look toward the front door. "What can I take out for you?"

And here it was again, her life rolling forward like a loose tumbleweed. "There's a small trunk on my bed. I can bring the carpetbag."

Willem nodded and disappeared down the hall. Edna turned to Fay. "I shouldn't go. You've so much to do here, with extra men to feed, and Lachlan isn't feeling well. No doubt your family needs Hugh to help while Lachlan is abed."

Fay put a hand on Edna's arm, effectively stopping her ramblings. "Hugh will make more money transporting you to Billings than he would staying home and caring for the animals. The farm is a manageable size now. Mama and I can do most of it, and Hugh will be back tomorrow night."

"I thought…" But Edna didn't say more, because experience had taught her that arguing with Fay was futile. Willem returned with her trunk in hand.

Edna gave her friend a hug and followed him out to the waiting coach. Hugh stood at the front of the coach, tall and handsome as ever. She was glad they were taking the coach and not a wagon. This way she would ride in silence alone and not have to stare at him or engage in conversation, knowing he loved another. It might have been nice to pretend. A little imagination to carry with her when she next faced Brandon.

Hugh opened the coach door, and Edna almost laughed at the formality of it. One might think she was a lady deserving of such gestures. Then, as though to quell any misconceptions, Hugh pulled a pistol from a pouch along the inside of the door and flipped the inner chamber out, giving it a spin.

He snapped it back together and met Edna's eyes. "Don't touch that."

Edna barked out a laugh. "I was hoping to use it for a bit of target practice on the way."

Hugh gave her a mock glare and stepped out of sight. Edna stared at the bulge of the gun in the pocket. If she hadn't known it was there, the shape would only look like a bit of stuffing. She leaned away from it. She was not yet comfortable enough with guns to tote one the way Fay did whenever she went into town without male company. When the coach door clicked closed, she found herself encased in fine damask and small glass windows, muffling the sounds outside. She could make out the different tone of each man's voice. Willem, then Hugh. Then the cabin shifted as Hugh climbed into the driving seat.

Soon they lurched forward and were off. Edna didn't look at the house, afraid if she looked back, it would be akin to a goodbye. She would return. She would be strong against whatever Brandon wanted.

Her life out here was good. And Fay had the right of it. If she waited long enough, she would find a man either in Dragonfly Creek or in the many wealthier men staying at the ranch for pleasure. Or even Hugh. She could hear him whistling on the other side of the wood, though she couldn't identify the tune. He and Catherine hadn't gotten together yet. Why not? Was Catherine *too good* for Hugh? Edna's indignation only reared for a second, for she couldn't blame a practical stranger for not wanting to marry a poor man. Just because Edna thought him fine and his family wonderful didn't mean every girl should want to wed a man so tied to his family's needs.

She shook her head free of her aimless wonderings and opened her carpet bag to finish the muff she'd started making for her mother. As she fingered the soft fur, she couldn't help but think how Hugh had refused her payment and instead gifted her the pelt. He was always doing that, being too kind to her. It was no wonder she found herself longing for the man leading the coach. A wall between them wasn't enough to take her mind off him. Perhaps hundreds of miles would do the trick.

IT HAD BEEN RAINING for an eternity, with no end in sight. Hugh's hat brim had turned floppy and did a poor job of shielding his face from the heavy drops. The roads were slick with mud, but the team maneuvered just fine, and he didn't want to stop until they'd reached a town.

Rather than sit in misery, he tried to imagine himself at home in the chair next to Pa, with a fire warming his limbs. If the temperature dropped, they might have a white Christmas. He would do well to head straight home after dropping Edna in Billings rather than stay the night in town. He could drive as far as was safe, then sleep in the coach overnight. It would be cold and uncomfortable, especially for the horses, but it might be the only way to avoid being stuck in Billings until the roads were usable.

He shook his head, thinking of the woman who sat in comfort behind him. They should have left for Billings last week. Why did he get the feeling Edna didn't want to go home for Christmas? He wished it had been him and not Willem who told her the arrangements had been made. He'd liked to have seen her face. What would he have seen? Gladness? Hesitation? If so, why? He'd known of men who ran from their pasts. His brother-in-law was one of them. But he'd yet to meet a lady doing the same. Perhaps there was family discord due to Edna leaving their family bakery and taking the job with Willem. Would her mother not welcome her back into their home? Hugh couldn't imagine a mother doing such a thing.

Hugh's thoughts followed this vein, due to both curiosity and boredom. As he mused, he squinted into the rain. A dark figure bounded through the rain at a gallop. Hugh's heart thudded in his chest as he tried to judge the rider's intent. He leaned forward, lifting the rifle from where it lay under the bench. The road was too slippery for him to hold the reins between his knees, so he kept one hand on the trigger and the other on the reins. He rested the barrel on his forearm and shouted at the rider. "Move off!"

The rain's steady pounding swallowed the man's reply. If he even made one. Another rider came from the other side. *Ambush.* Hugh fired the rifle at the first man and spun to aim another shot at the newcomer. He squeezed the trigger, but his jerky movements had confused the horses, and the coach veered to the right, bumping along the shoulder of the dirt road. Hugh dropped the rifle onto the floor and straightened out the team, though what he wanted to do was attempt to outrun these bandits. He resisted the reflex. If the coach tipped, both he and Edna would be badly hurt, or killed, and they'd be left as fodder for these bandits.

Handling the horses had taken too much of Hugh's attention and now the bandits were upon them. A third rider appeared behind the first man, his gun trained on Hugh. The first two riders closed together in front of Hugh's team of horses. No matter that Hugh snapped the reins, the horses had no choice but to slow with the riders. Hugh dropped the reins and reloaded the rifle just as the wagon came to a stop.

When he looked up, the rider closest to him had his gun raised, the barrel aimed between Hugh's eyes. He could almost see down the barrel and into the man's black heart.

"Drop the gun." The man had a long blond beard stained with tobacco juice, visible even in this downpour. The three men hadn't bothered to cover their faces. Either it was too wet to breathe through a bandana, or they had little to lose. He prayed it was the damp. He lowered the gun to the floor and sat up again with his palms exposed.

Beard jerked his chin at Hugh's waist. "Your other gun."

Hugh gritted his teeth as he pulled the pistol from the holster at his waist. The rifle was Willem's; he could afford another. The pistol was Hugh's, only one of two their family owned. He eyed the gun as it transferred hands. Why should he consider the cost of replacing a pistol when he was as likely to be dead within the hour?

The first rider, recognizable because of his light buckskin mount, came near. "How many you got in there?"

Hugh still had his hands high, his breathing ragged as two pistols pointed at his face. "Just one, and we ain't got much. Just one employee taking another to Billings so she can have Christmas with her family."

The bandit's eyes narrowed. "We'll see. Tell her to exit the coach."

Hugh flexed his jaw at the idea of Edna being anywhere near these men.

Beard pulled the hammer back. The faint click called little attention to the deathly blow that would occur with the slightest movement of the man's trigger finger.

Hugh raised his hands. "I'll get her." He climbed down slowly, hoping to come across as compliant and get out of this with all his blood still inside. He stared at the door, wishing this had been one of the times he was taking an empty coach to Billings instead of one with a lone woman.

Everything about this trip was wrong. Perhaps Edna's unwillingness to go was because she had a sense for bad luck.

With a heavy hand, Hugh gripped the handle and tugged, revealing Edna, curled in the corner, her face twisted with horror. Edna's eyes were wide and she took a shuddering breath as though her fear had subsided at the sight of him.

"We're in trouble. Do everything I say, when I say it." His words were quiet and quick. He motioned with his head, then raised his voice so the men could hear. "Come on out." Hugh reached into the hidden pocket on the coach door and pulled the pistol from its belly. He met Edna's gaze, wishing he had something clever to say, something to ease her worry, but his tongue was tied in knots. Instead, he held a hand out to help her from the coach. She took it, her knuckles white as she clung to him. Clutching her carpet bag in her other hand, she stepped down.

With the door blocking them from view, Hugh caught Edna by the back of her belt and tucked the pistol between it and her body, covering it with her shawl. She sucked in a breath, holding still until he'd finished the job.

Beard approached and Hugh shifted Edna behind him, allowing the man to pass. Instead, Beard shoved Hugh out of the way and crawled inside the coach. Its springs squeaked with his weight. Hugh noticed the brown stains the man left on the seat and hardly cared. The coach was as good as gone. These men were after the horses, and the coach was a nice bonus.

Buckskin rode his horse closer and tossed Edna a slimy smile. "Headed home for Christmas, eh? Let's see what you've got in that bag of yours."

Edna shrank into Hugh's side, clutching her bag tighter. Hugh wrapped an arm around her shoulders and whispered, "They'll take it anyway." He reached down and took the weight of her bag in his arms, giving her time to loosen her grip and release it. When she did, Hugh thrust it toward the leader.

The buckskin leader jerked his head at the second man, who was marked with a large red blotch on his face, more like a mark he'd been born with rather than something earned in a fight. The marked man climbed off his horse and strode closer, snagging the bag from Hugh. All the while, the leader's gun remained trained in Hugh and Edna's direction.

Hugh prayed the man had steady fingers.

The marked man opened the bag and pulled out its contents—first the fur Hugh had given her, and then Edna's undergarments, which he tossed onto the muddy ground one at a time. Hugh still had an arm around Edna, and he squeezed her, offering comfort in any small way because he didn't dare speak.

Beard tumbled about in the coach still, making it rock behind them. The marked man rummaged through Edna's belongings, gun sitting on the muddy ground, forgotten. Only the leader's focus remained on them, and Hugh knew he'd have no better chance than this.

He removed his hand from Edna's shoulder and tugged the pistol from her belt. With quick hands he pulled the hammer back, not caring if the man heard the noise, and pointed it at the leader first. He shot and the man fell from his horse. The beast shuddered and pranced away, but it must have been used to such commotion, for it didn't go much farther. Hugh turned to the carpetbag man, who had dropped the bag but was feeling his empty holster for his gun. Hugh shot him as well, and the man fell back, clutching his shoulder.

Hugh spun and trained his gun at the coach, but the door was closed now, the third man was nowhere to be seen. He'd probably ducked within the coach, but with such a hiding place he had the advantage, and danger still surrounded them.

"To the horse." Hugh shoved Edna toward the buckskin horse still nearby. The two other horses were racing, stirrups flapping, into the forest. He turned back to the two men on the ground. The leader clutched at his shoulder as blood oozed between his fingers. The other was curled on his side so Hugh couldn't see his face. He lay still. Hugh rounded the horse and plucked the leader's gun from the muddy earth. Then he collected the marked man's gun where it lay next to Edna's discarded personals. With a grunt he mounted onto the horse behind Edna.

"Hold tight," he told her. He sent a shot toward the coach before digging his heels into the horse's flank.

He whipped the horse's rear with the reins, urging it faster. A gunshot sounded, followed by a shudder and the scream of the horse beneath them. Two more shots pierced the air. Pain seared in Hugh's shoulder, but he curved his body around Edna, praying he was large enough to block her from any bullets. He veered into the forest, fully aware there could be any number of bandits lying in wait in the trees. He kept the horse's pace, trusting it to weave through the trees. Branches whipped at their faces, and Hugh knew Edna was taking more hits than he, but they couldn't stop.

They rode deeper into the forest, until the horse began to trip and stumble. Hugh slowed the beast, scanning the forest for landmarks to find his bearings. Rain pelted them and the sun was barely visible. Nevertheless, he could see its subtle brightness, telling him they'd gone north.

He'd hunted all over these hills; he could gauge how close they were to Trapper Pete's cabin. The world lurched around him as the horse struggled to stay on its feet. He gripped the reins in one hand and wrapped his other arm around Edna as the horse stumbled, rocking their bodies forward, and fell to its knees. Hugh slid his feet from the stirrups and swung Edna off, following himself before his foot could be pinned between the earth and the dying animal. The beast collapsed to its side with a great sigh, eyes wide and rolling.

Hugh looked around to see how much distance they'd put between themselves and their enemies. There was no way to tell. The bandits could have unhitched Willem's horses or found their own. At least one of them was likely on Hugh and Edna's trail now. He removed the saddlebag from the horse's flanks and flung it over his shoulder. He moved away, but stopped when Edna tugged the cuff of his sleeve.

He turned to find her staring at the horse, lying on its side, its chest heaving. "We can't leave it like this." The storm wet her face, but her twisted expression turned rain drops to tears.

Hugh squeezed Edna's wrist. "We can't risk a gunshot. They'll hear. They'll find us."

She planted her feet and threw her shoulders back. "It saved our lives. We cannot leave it to the wolves."

She was right. The blood would draw predators, and the horse would suffer a gruesome death. But a gunshot wasn't an option. "It's not worth dying for." Hugh turned, but Edna pulled the knife from his hip as slick as if he'd removed it himself.

Hugh almost laughed. "That blade is not large enough to kill the horse. He'd just kick out and break your leg or mine."

Edna's eyes filled with tears. "We can't *leave* him."

She hugged herself, the blade sticking helplessly into the damp air at her side. His shoulder ached with every heartbeat he could hear in his ears. The pain and the blood wetting his shirt told him they were in trouble if they didn't find Pete's soon. "Edna, we have to find a place to sleep. We cannot waste time waiting for the beast to die. We need to get far away from here or the wolves will come for us, too."

Her wide, fearful eyes met his, then her gaze fell on the front of his shirt. Her brows drew together, and she blinked, but when her eyes opened, they were locked on his bloody shirt once more. "You're hurt. When...?"

He glanced down, surprised at how much it had bled. He wasn't new to injury and blood, but this was the first time he'd been shot. The bullet had torn through him as though he were little more than a piece of parchment. "I need to get out of these trees so I can see where we are."

Edna raised a hand and let her fingers hover over his wound, as though wishing she could heal him with a spell. She looked down, grief flicking on her face, then steeled herself and met his eyes with a nod.

He shifted the saddlebag higher and turned to Edna. "You ready for a hike?"

She nodded, lifting her gaze toward the treetops and away from the dying creature. He moved up the hill, praying he would find a meadow or clearing so he could see beyond the tall trees.

They found something even better. A stream. He stopped and cupped his hands to drink. Edna did the same.

He watched her. "Are you doing alright?"

Edna nodded as she wiped water from her chin with her sleeve. She was quiet. Too quiet. In the months she'd been in Aster Ridge, he'd grown accustomed to her being ready with banter or a teasing word.

He pointed north. "There's a trapper out here named Pete. His place isn't far. If we follow this stream for a while, I think we can find it."

Edna stood and looked around her. She appeared out of place here in the merciless forest. Even with her hair plastered to her face and her teeth chattering, she had a warmth and a regal bearing that made her seem more part of a city drawing room than part of anything wild and dangerous.

She'd barely begun to fit in at Aster Ridge, and now she was deeper into the wilderness. Deep in trouble. For, in this remote section of forest, Hugh was likely not the only one who knew about Pete's cabin.

"We should keep moving."

"Yeah." Edna's voice was a whisper, but she'd spoken, which was a comfort.

He reached out and took her hand. "We'll move a bit slower." Not just for her sake, but because his shoulder throbbed worse than the time a horse had stepped on and broken his big toe.

Edna's fingers curled around his. "No. Night is falling. We should move as fast as we can." She tugged on the saddlebag. "Let me carry that. You're injured."

Hugh reached with his free hand to tug it bag back from her and immediately regretted the movement. He sucked in a sharp breath and nearly whimpered at the pain exploding in his shoulder.

Edna faced him and cupped her palms over his cheeks, her fingers settling gently against his skin. "Let me help you." Then her eyes changed from concerned to mischievous. "I don't think you'll be able to put up much of a fight."

Hugh glared. "You would take advantage of a crippled man?"

"When he's being stubborn."

Hugh used his good arm to adjust the position of the saddlebag. "It's fine on this shoulder, and luckily it's quite heavy. If we don't find Pete's soon, we can stop and see what food is in here."

Edna pursed her lips, but started walking.

Hugh wanted to take her hand again, to feel the smooth pads of her fingers against his skin. Instead, he focused on the trees and the land leading them in the direction of Pete's cabin.

8

DESPITE BEING SHOT, Hugh kept a surprisingly hurried pace. By the time he slowed to a stop, Edna was ready to lie down on the earth and sleep for a full day. She looked up, seemingly for the first time in hours, to find a rustic cabin before them, hard to make out in the dark forest. If they'd been one hour later, the forest would have been so black they might have walked right past the house and not seen it.

Light splotches on the roof caught her gaze. She stared for a moment before she realized they were antlers. Her stomach rumbled at the thought of meat. Funny, she could still recall the first time she'd seen Bastien dress a deer carcass, the bloody mess had turned her stomach. Now, that sight would have made her salivate with the prospect of fresh meat. She hoped this Pete was prepared for guests.

Hugh approached the door, which had boards laid across it, resting in squarish sort of hooks. Hugh set the boards aside, wincing with each one, and reached for the handle.

"Wait!" Edna whispered, glancing at the darkening forest behind them. "What are you *doing*?"

Hugh smirked at her. "Did you want to sleep outside?"

She glanced around the clearing. A small, dilapidated barn stood as though waiting for the wind and rain to turn it into firewood. It would as soon collapse on them as it would provide alternative shelter. Outside in the bitter cold, with wolves prowling around? She shuddered. Rain pattered on her hair, reminding her the wolves weren't the only element she would be contending with. She'd begun to wonder whether it rained more in the trees, as though the tall ponderosas possessed the ability to hold the clouds in place and demand to be watered. But manners got the better of her. "We can't just enter a person's home without permission."

"It's that or the ground." Hugh ducked his head to look at the sky beyond the porch's roof. "We can pray the rain turns to snow. Do you want to take *your* chances inside or out?"

Edna glowered at him. She didn't miss the way he said 'your' as though he weren't going to accompany her if she chose the outdoors. Somehow, she felt like an idiot for attempting the simple courtesy of not breaking into someone's home. "In Chicago, the police arrest folks for doing this exact thing." Nevertheless, she climbed the steps and stood behind him.

Hugh chuckled as he pushed open the door. "Out west, we *are* the police. Pete will shoot us if he wants and nobody will be the wiser."

Edna's feet froze in the doorway, not daring to step further. She spoke with a dry mouth. "Shoot us?"

Hugh groaned and flopped the saddle bag onto a table with intricately carved legs. He pulled out the water skin and offered it to Edna, but she couldn't break the hold those swirls had on her. Such a delicate detail on such a brutal day. The contrast tried to overwhelm her.

"Edna…. Edna." Hugh dipped into her vision, breaking the hold the carvings had over her. "Edna, I was only teasing about Pete. He's a friend and he's not here. You have nothing to worry about."

Edna barked a hard laugh. "Nothing to worry about." She met his gaze, stepping closer so he took a step back. "What about when he returns and shoots us both? I might rather take my chances with the wolves."

"Best case, you'll get chilblains." Hugh returned to the saddlebag, opening up the other side. With a clatter, several metal bullets rolled out and onto the floor. "Fools. No wonder they're robbing folks. They haven't the sense to pack more than lead."

Edna went to it and covered the opening with her hand. "We can't stay here."

Hugh winced and rolled his shoulder.

Edna eyed him, trying to read his face to see if he was using pity to distract her. He'd never been one to complain, though. "Does it hurt badly?"

Hugh raised his eyebrows and cocked his head. "Have you ever been shot?"

Edna drew herself as high as she could. "No. I do my best to stay away from those types of folks, which is precisely why I'd like to leave." Chicago had its share of thugs, who looked nothing like those bandits. They wore suits and did their evil deeds in the shadows.

Hugh turned and opened a cupboard along the wall. He pulled down a tin and tried opening it with his good hand. "Pete is a friend. So long as he recognizes me before he pulls his gun, we'll be fine."

That did ease her worries a bit. Edna took the tin from his hands. "Stop it. Will you go lie down? I'll see if your *friend* has any herbs to help that wound."

Edna peeled her wet jacket off and hung it on a peg by the door. She helped Hugh do the same and took up the chore of raiding a stranger's cupboards. Edna's familiarity with herbs meant she knew a thing or two about which ones were medicinal. The problem was that she'd never had the need to use her knowledge. Frederick's family had always been nearby whenever her or Mama were sick. Edna's heart pricked at the memory of her old friend, of all the friends she'd lost due to Brandon.

Edna found a wooden dish, the top and sides carved as beautifully as the table legs. She opened it and the scent of calendula hit her. Edna dipped her finger in and pulled it out, sliding her fingertips together with a smile. It was already made into a salve. Whoever this Pete was, he was wise enough to have either purchased a salve or rendered one himself.

She crossed the cabin, the planks echoing beneath her boots. Hugh was blowing into the black-bellied stove, the orange glow within lighting his face. He kept his bad arm tucked into his stomach, and with his other one, he placed a large piece of wood in the stove.

With the calendula in one hand, she pressed her free fist into her waist. "I can finish this. Go lie down."

He pulled a small bit of wood from the stove; a flame flickered at the end. He used it to light the lantern at his side, then tossed the wood back into the stove and closed the door. He stood, lantern in hand. Wounded as he was, he was still taller than her and so broad it was a wonder he could be hurt by anything at all.

She followed him to the bed and waited while he struggled to remove his boots with one hand. Edna set down the dish of calendula and knelt on the wooden floor at his feet. She gripped the heel and toe of his boot and tugged, using what little strength she had left from walking in the wet and cold. The boot came off and Edna fell backward, the muddy boot landing on her dress. She sat forward to look at the mess.

Hugh offered her a hand, a hint of laughter on his lips, but she waved it away. "May as well do the other one while I'm already filthy."

They got his other boot off with less fanfare, and then Edna pushed Hugh back onto the pillow. "Let me see your shoulder, cowboy."

He raised his gaze, and this close she could see the whites of his eyes were red. Whether due to the wind or something else, she couldn't tell. He straightened, only the hitch in his breath giving him away. He tried to lift his shirt with one hand.

Edna clicked her tongue. "Let's not be concerned with modesty." She pulled at his shirt, fully untucking it from his trousers, and tugged the blood-soaked material over his head. She gasped, as the wound looked much worse than when it was hidden beneath blood-soaked cloth, and a thin trail of blood still leaked from the damaged flesh. She pressed the already ruined shirt to his wound, earning a wince from him. "I'm sorry. I have a salve, but I have to clean it first, and it has to stop bleeding before I can clean it."

Hugh nodded. She'd never known him to be chatty like his sister, but he was quieter than usual now. She should get him tucked into bed as soon as possible. And make him a bit of grub. Who knew how long he would sleep after a bullet wound and an exhaustingly long walk through a dense forest?

Frederick had once suggested the use of alcohol to clean a wound. She glanced around the cabin. Hopefully this Pete was a drinking fellow.

She took Hugh's good hand and laid it over the shirt, balled up against his wound. "Hold this for a moment."

She went to the cupboard again and rifled through various tins. Nothing liquid. They might have to settle for the skin of water, which was nearly out. She'd have to fill it first, which was a good idea seeing as how the light of the day was nearly gone.

She lifted the skin from the pile of items on the table. Too much to do all at once. Feed the fire. Fill the water skin. Clean Hugh's wound. Possibly sew the wound shut. Make a bit of food. Clean their clothes, or at least hang them to dry. Her heart beat with every item added to the list. First water, before full darkness fell and she had to venture out into the woods with the wolves and bears.

She made for the door, and just as her hand reached the latch, Hugh's voice came, gravelly, and the pain in it took away Edna's breath. "Where are you going?"

"Just out to fill this skin." A bucket caught her eye, and she grabbed it. "And this pot." Better to have too much than too little.

Hugh sat up, his face twisted in agony. "I'll go."

Edna made her best serious face and said, "I'm just going to the stream. I'll be right back."

Hugh held her gaze for a moment, and Edna expected him to argue, but instead he let out a puff of air and leaned back again.

Edna took her chance to hustle out and fill the skin. Darkness hadn't totally fallen, but everything was cloaked in black, like the inside of an empty fireplace. The trees were no longer green and brown, just dark and darker. Even the water was an inky black in the ground. She found a large rock and held the skin to catch the water that ran off of it. Next was the pot. The icy water made her fingers ache, and once she'd filled the containers, she dried her hands on her skirts, then breathed on them to take away some of the chill.

When she entered the house again, Hugh looked the same as when she'd left. His eyes were closed, but he spoke. "Can you replace the beams that go across the door?"

Edna turned toward the closed door. "Why?"

"I'm not sure whether Pete used them when he was here or only when he was away. That latch isn't strong enough to hold back a grizzly."

Edna's heart kicked in her chest. She pulled open the door, her eyes scanning the dark. She'd just been out there alone in the dark and now she was barring the door against bears. Standing in the open doorway, she stacked the lowest beam first, hooking it into the wooden bracket.

As she stacked each plank, the opening closed until the entrance was barred by planks hooked onto the exterior wall of the cabin. She shut and latched the door, then turned to place the pot on the flat surface of the stove. The little thing had begun to put off a bit of heat. She added another log to the inside and shut the door once more. The fire sent a ripple of heat across the room that comforted her bones. It also promised she'd be feeding the stove wood through the whole night if she let it burn so hot, so she adjusted the damper. Behind the stove, she discovered a rack Pete must use to dry clothes. She added *set up rack* to her mental list.

She placed her fists onto her waist. "I'm warming some water so I can clean your shoulder. Where would Pete keep a bit of alcohol?"

Hugh's eyes stayed closed. "Probably makes it himself. Top cupboard maybe, or under the bed?" His voice sounded tight and thick with pain.

Under the bed. Brilliant. Edna knelt on the floor by Hugh's stockinged foot. She avoided looking at it, for his socks were sure to be as sodden as her own. His other foot rested up on the bed. She groped in the dark, finding only a thick layer of dust, but then her fingers brushed something cool—glass. She moved farther under the bed, her whole head and shoulder underneath, until she got hold of the neck of whatever bottle she'd found.

She popped back up with a smile. Something sloshed

inside when she pulled the bottle upright. She worked at the cork, using her teeth at one point, until it opened. The smell of alcohol almost bowled her over and she gave a small cough. "Found it," she squeaked.

"Pour me a tall glass." Hugh's voice was tight. Edna hadn't meant it for Hugh to drink, but she wasn't about to refuse a man barely holding it together. She poured a full cup and went to Hugh. "Drink it slowly. There's nothing in your stomach."

Hugh opened his eyes and took the cup from her hands. "Pete must have some jerky here."

Edna nodded, adding *find jerky* to her growing list. "Slowly, if you please." The last thing she needed on her list was *deal with a large drunk man*.

Hugh's eyes were closed again, and he had a small smile on his lips. She adjusted the wick and lit the lantern, taking it over and setting it on the small table beside the bed. "Let's get you more comfortably settled before you're not able to move at all."

Hugh shifted more fully on the bed and winced, lifting his other leg up too. She cocked her head. He was at the edge and on top of all the quilts, rather than under them, but he didn't seem to mind. As for herself, she'd love to burrow down into that bed and warm herself to the bone.

Instead, she set Hugh's boots near the stove to dry and worked the buttons so she could step out of her own shoes. They were not only wet, but mud had worked its way between the buttons. Brandon's family made fine shoes, but these particular ones weren't intended for gallivanting through a rain-soaked forest. The boots would serve better as fodder for the fire at this point. She almost consigned them to the flames, but stayed her hand at the last moment. Flimsy or not, they were all she had. She'd need them a bit longer. If they didn't die out here, she would be tramping through these woods again.

Next, Edna searched the kitchen tins for flour and soda, hoping to get a bit of grub in Hugh's belly before he fell asleep. She found jerky and traded Hugh for his cup of spirits. She frowned. He'd drunk more than half and lay relaxed and still, smiling as he chewed the dried meat.

"You're drunk." Edna couldn't hide the laughter in her voice.

"I can still feel the hole in my shoulder, so I figure I'm not drunk enough."

Edna took the cup back to the cupboard. "That's enough until I get a bit more food in you."

"You make good food."

She smiled as she searched the cupboards. At last, she found soda, but still no flour. She tapped her first finger on her bottom lip, looking around the space. The cabin was small and flour would be something he kept a large amount of. Unless he was out of the stuff, and that's where he was— on a supply run. But no, if he were out, she'd have found an empty container. Just then, her gaze fell on a large crock, a twin to the one that held kindling. This one had a lid though. She lifted it and found flour.

A wave of relief came, but was just as quickly followed by anxiety. She used the water, flour and soda to mix up a bland dough. As she stirred, stress rose in her throat, threatening to choke her.

She shouldn't be here now. She should be warm in a hotel, waiting to board a train home to Chicago where there was law and order. A glance at Hugh told her he was content, even with a hole in his shoulder, but he wouldn't be fit to do any more traipsing through the woods. And there was only the smallest amount of food to get them through. How long would they last here before they starved? If the door holds against a bear, what of the wolves? And if animals aren't the problem, the owner of this cabin might well shoot them, or the men who robbed the coach could come to finish what they'd begun.

Edna pressed her palms flat against her stomach. She slowed her breathing, knowing panic wasn't the answer. With a deep breath, she pushed the thoughts as far away as she could and focused on finishing their meal. Food, in the form of a bakery, had been the solution when her papa died. If it could solve a problem like that, surely it would help her now.

9

FINALLY THE CABIN had warmed and their bellies were full of burnt pancakes. Edna wanted to lie down and sleep for a week, but Hugh was not yet stitched up.

She stood and checked the water on the stove. It was warm enough that it wouldn't shock him when she cleaned the blood from his chest. She dipped a rag in and wrung it out.

Edna went to Hugh and lifted the shirt, but it had dried to the wound. She wanted to curse her foolishness. She should have tended the wound before anything else. "I'm sorry," she said as she wiped at the stuck edges of the shirt. She took the scabs with it and the blood started again. This wound seemed intent on letting her start over as many times as she needed.

Once the shirt was free, she dabbed at the blood with the rag. Hugh hadn't yet moved to the middle of the bed, so she was able to reach him easily. She sat on the sliver of bed between him and the edge and cleaned the rest of his skin, as low as she dared. The blood reached below the waistband of his trousers and she had her limits.

At last his chest and stomach were clean and the wound was done oozing. Hugh was relaxed into the bed, but Edna knew his back would be in similar shape to his front. Dried blood and the other half of the wound. Best to get this side finished so she could work on the other.

Edna got the cup of spirits and laid the rag under the wound to catch whatever ran down his chest. She tried to remember if this was right. Maybe Frederick hadn't meant for it to be used on the outside, only the inside. Hugh had begun smiling almost as soon as he started drinking, so maybe she was wrong and the inside was what counted. But what difference would it make? If this didn't work, they'd be no worse off. And his wound was open, so maybe if she poured it so it went inside...

Hugh's eyes bulged, followed by a roar. He was barely on the bed and his quick movement knocked the cup of alcohol from her hands. She was too stunned to get her feet under her before she fell off the bed, followed by Hugh. He cracked his head on the side table and the lantern wobbled precariously before righting itself. Edna sighed and began untangling her legs from Hugh's.

He groaned, holding at his shoulder. Blood oozed between his fingers as he clutched the wound in pain.

Edna abandoned her attempts to free her skirts from under Hugh and tried her best to pry his fingers away, knowing he was hurting himself and making the opening worse. "I'm sorry. I'm so sorry. I didn't know it would hurt." She wasn't cut out for this. She was going to kill him by trying to fix him with vague memories from a lifetime ago. She wished Frederick were here with her now. He'd know all the things to do to fix Hugh up and Hugh wouldn't be bleeding for the fourth time today.

Hugh finally released his shoulder and used his good arm

to prop himself up. His eyes were dark as he leveled her with a look. "What…was… that?" he panted.

"Spirits. I…they're used to clean a wound."

Hugh took a deep breath. "Don't do it again."

Edna shook her head vigorously. "I won't." She was still pinned much too close to him, unable to move away until he lifted his bottom half off the folds of her skirt.

Hugh squinted at Edna, no doubt wondering what she was doing with her face so close to his. Then he glanced up at the bed. "Did I fall?"

Edna bit her lips to keep from laughing. "More like you tackled me for my mistake."

Hugh's gaze, which was surveying their predicament, flew to meet Edna's. "I didn't."

The laugh she'd been suppressing bubbled out of her, expelling any awkwardness she was feeling at being nearly beneath him. She laughed now and tugged at his good arm. "Let's get you tucked into bed, cowboy."

Hugh raised to sitting, but stopped. "I can't sleep there. Where will you sleep?"

She still had hold of his arm and scoffed as she pulled at it. He didn't move. She might be able to heft a sack of flour, but he weighed a bit more. "I'm sure I'll be safe. You're hardly in any condition to take advantage."

He looked at her, his eyes having lost all the calmness from the alcohol. "I'll not compromise you."

"I appreciate the thought, but I've already seen one mouse and I'm not sleeping on the floor."

"Edna." His tone was a warning and the lantern light showed his eyes were still bloodshot. She had an over-whelming urge to tend him. To tuck him into bed and brush that wavy hair from his brow.

He jerked his head toward the bed. "Pass me some blankets." He raised his good arm so it was under his head like a pillow. Edna caught herself staring at his torso and turned away. "I can't go anywhere until you move off my dress."

He glanced down and smirked. With a grunt, he lifted himself off the fabric. He closed his eyes. "When the men in Dragonfly Creek said nobody could pin you down, I don't think they meant this."

The men in Dragonfly Creek had talked to Hugh about her? Edna stood, shaking out her skirts. Pete might have medicines, but his floors had been sorely neglected. She grimaced to think of Hugh's bare back and open wound on such a floor. "I still have to tend the back of your shoulder."

Hugh opened one eye. "You'll have to get me another glass of that fire whiskey if you want to do anything more."

Edna obliged, filling another cup and holding it out to him. He reached up from the floor but she held it back. "I'm not sitting on that floor again until I've given it a good scrubbing."

"I'm injured. Quit making me move to and fro." He added a grimace, as though that would convince her.

Edna gestured him forward with her hand and, despite his words, he lifted himself to sitting and took Edna's hand. He tugged at it, causing her to stumble toward him. He laughed, squinting at her with one eye. "I still don't think you can heft a sack of flour."

Edna tugged hard on his arm and he lifted off the ground. "You're a bit heavier."

Hugh turned to climb into the bed and Edna gasped at the dirt that now covered his back. "Oh, Hugh. You're filthy."

He turned his face as though trying to see his own back. "Clean me up, doc."

Edna huffed. "I'm as likely to kill you as cure you."

Hugh shrugged. "Sounds like a doctor to me."

The air in the room changed. Edna knew Hugh's family had a tragic history with the success of doctors. They had spent most of their lives with an invalid for a father and, more recently, a sick elder brother who had no hope for a full recovery. "Can you stay like this while I clean your back?"

"Pass me that cup first. I'm not sure I trust you with spirits anymore."

Edna smiled and pressed the cup into his hands. He took two large gulps and covered his mouth with his wrist as he coughed and sucked in a breath. "Those are the worst spirits I've ever tasted. I can't tell if it's too old or too new."

Edna dipped the rag in the now very hot water and opened it so the cold air could cool it down before wringing it out. She came back to stand behind Hugh and started at the top of his back, running the wet cloth over his broad shoulders. Goose pimples rose across the expanse and Edna spoke in hopes of distracting him. "What do you know about making whiskey? Are you in the habit of bootlegging?"

Hugh's shoulders shook and his laugh was soft. "Lach and I have tried to make a bit of our own. It tastes about as bad as this stuff."

"I think you're better off. I've known plenty of men who like it a bit too much." In truth, it was the wives of such men she had known. Bent and bruised, they were.

Edna dabbed at the entrance wound from the bullet. It was smaller than the exit at the front and she squinted at it, wondering if there would even be the need for a stitch. Perhaps just a bandage would do.

She took the calendula and smeared a generous amount over the opening. Then she covered it with a square of fabric she'd found in another dish stored on the same shelf as the calendula. The cloth had been accompanied by a bit of thread and a needle.

Holding the square in place, she tapped on his shoulder. "I can't wrap it yet, not until I've stitched the front."

He turned and, in order to hold the fabric to his wound, she had to move with him and practically hug him. She kept her eyes away from his, staring instead at the dip at the base of his neck. Even that bit of innocent flesh had her gulping down embarrassment. "If you'll just lie back, the pressure will hold this in place." And eventually the dry blood. Would she make it bleed again when she went to change the bandage in the morning?

Edna switched hands so her arm wasn't around his back, but she still had to climb onto the bed with him and hold it until he was situated.

When she finally leaned back, her knees still touched his side. A satisfied smile stretched his face.

"What are you smiling about?"

"I can't seem to forget what the men in Dragonfly Creek would be thinking if they could see us now."

They'd think Hugh had quite the adventure. But none of them liked Edna enough to care that she'd been alone with Hugh for an extended period of time. "I wonder what Catherine Price would think."

Hugh tensed and Edna held back a smirk of her own. *So he doesn't like his own medicine. Interesting.* She climbed over his legs and off the bed, then tucked blankets around him, covering everything but the top bit of his wounded shoulder. If the bullet had hit lower, it would have caught the bone and knocked Hugh from the saddle. He'd probably have taken Edna down with him, and who knew what those bandits would have done to them.

Edna nodded at the cup. "Have the rest. The worst part is here." She turned and collected the needle and thread. She considered running it through alcohol, but didn't dare, not with the way Hugh was watching her every move. It was like he didn't trust her anymore. She was surprised he'd even let his guard down enough to finish the alcohol in his cup.

He endured the stitching with little more than sharp intakes of breath and clenched fists. Once the job was done, she did the same as before, smearing it with calendula and covering it with a square of fabric.

Edna tried to retuck the blankets around his chin, but Hugh caught her hand. "You know my mother would have my neck if she knew I slept on the bed with you."

Edna scoffed. "Stop. I've plenty to do in this little cabin. If it's so important, I'll let you sleep for a bit and when I'm ready for sleep, I'll wake you to move onto the floor."

Edna turned so he couldn't read her face. She had no intention of moving him to the floor. Nor did she intend to make the floor ready for her to sleep. They would share the bed. At the rate he was consuming spirits, he wouldn't wake up until long after morning. He would probably sleep until the afternoon and wake with a pounding headache.

10

HUGH WOKE to radiating pain in his shoulder. He winced and slowly lifted his good arm to cup his wrecked shoulder. Rather than his fingers brushing bandaged skin, his hand found something else. Edna.

The rising sun lent scant light to the cabin's interior, and Hugh discovered she'd not only slept in the bed with him, but her body was flush against his, her face resting on his bandaged shoulder.

He tried to move out from under her, but the pain was too much. Instead, he used his good arm to gently roll her away from him as he slid out of the bed. When he turned back he noted a bit of dried blood on her cheek. He glanced down, his bare skin covered in chills and the cloth over his wound had a dark spot in the center.

He noted the spot on her face matched the shape, a souvenir for her treachery. No doubt her snuggle had caused his wound to bleed. It was a wonder he hadn't woken before dawn from the pain. And yet, she hadn't been afraid to share the bed. More, her face was smooth, as if the weight of the day had dissolved while she slept near him. What did she have to worry her so? He wanted answers. Why was she so hesitant to go home, but not so much that she would confide in anyone?

Hugh pulled his discarded and bloody shirt off the drying rack by the stove and slid it over his head. He walked to the window to find a blanket of snow, several inches thick, covered everything, softening each edge with downy white. He'd heard the rain in the night, and should have known the air would turn cold enough for that rain to become snow.

He leaned his forehead against the wooden window frame, the coolness soothing a touch of the headache that raged. His family would expect him home today. What would they do when he didn't arrive? What had happened to Willem's coach? Hugh's stomach churned and, for a moment, he thought he would be sick. There was no way they could walk home, not with snow up to their knees and no horse to carry them through. It was still falling in lazy flakes. He wondered how long until it would stop. How long could they wait to head out? Edna was right. Hugh didn't know for sure where Pete was or when he was returning. They needed him to get out of this pickle.

Hugh's family would be rattled. Edna's mother too. Unless Edna hadn't had time to tell her mama she was coming. If that was the case, nobody would miss her. That thought rankled him, made his neck tingle. Who was failing Edna? Why did it feel like she was alone in this big world?

Shaking his head, he made his way back to her. She'd moved into his spot, her head not even on her pillow anymore. He lifted the top two blankets off and made himself a bedroll on the floor. She might have climbed into bed with him last night, but she would surely regret such a scandalous decision in the light of the morning. Before he climbed into his makeshift bed, he threw another two logs into the stove.

He slept fitfully, troubled by the ache of his throbbing

shoulder. When Edna finally rose and began making noise, Hugh was glad to throw off the covers and begin rolling up his blankets.

Edna rushed over. "You shouldn't be doing that." She nudged him over and took the blanket from his hand.

"I'm not some porcelain doll to be broken."

She glanced at him over her shoulder, the blanket folded in her arms. "Only because I put you back together again last night."

Hugh laughed. She had a point. "Well, thanks to you, I'm better now."

She laid the folded blanket along the foot of the bed. "You're not fixed yet, Humpty Dumpty. I need to change your bandages this morning." Edna leaned against the bed, crossing her ankles. "What are we going to do? We can't stay here. It's not our home. And the food will run out eventually." She gulped. "They'll know you lost the coach. I'm so sorry. This is all my fault."

Hugh wanted to put an arm around her, to draw her close and tell her he didn't blame her for anything. Instead, he shoved his good hand into his pocket and said, "You didn't do anything, unless you hired those bandits to rob us."

She huffed in rueful amusement, but it didn't reach her eyes as she stared at the floor. "I should have let you take me sooner, when Lachlan was well. Or I should have refused to go and had Christmas with the Grahams. They're not a bad family to be around, you know."

"Not bad, no, but you should be with your mama for Christmas. I don't blame you for wanting to go home." He watched her. Waiting. But her face appeared serene and showed no resistance to going home.

Edna pressed away from the bed, rubbing her hands together. "I guess there will be no Christmas feast. All Pete has is flour and a bit of dried jerky."

"Have you checked the cellar?" Hugh highly doubted Pete would have let his supplies run down to just two ingredients.

Edna shook her head, looking about the space as though she'd merely missed it.

Hugh lifted her jacket from the peg and passed it to her. "Follow me."

She put it on and cast him a curious look as he led the way to Pete's root cellar, located a ways away due to his cabin's close proximity to the stream. "He had to put it over here. If it were close to the creek, it would be too damp and his goods would mold."

When they arrived, Hugh frowned. The door had a lock hanging from it. He tugged at the lock, but he'd been a fool to hope it wouldn't be secure. Hugh could just imagine all the food down there. Carrots, beets, onions, apples. It was still early enough that he might have preserved peaches and pears on the shelves.

Edna rubbed at her arms and looked around. "This will be my first full winter out here in Montana."

Hugh trudged back toward the house. "You were here last winter."

"I guess so. But that was the end of the season, when everyone was done with winter and praying for spring. This time, I'm here when we don't mind it so much."

They entered the cabin and Hugh rooted around every cup and corner, looking for the key. Pete probably kept it on him, but he was smart enough to have a backup key. Or perhaps he figured if he lost the one, he could ax down the door to the cellar. Hugh wasn't opposed to the idea. Only, with his shoulder, it would be no easy feat, and that didn't include the need to build Pete a new door.

He gave a low growl and flattened the palm of his good hand on the table.

Edna turned to him, wide-eyed from where she stood warming her hands at the fire.

He clenched his teeth, gesturing to the stove. "This stove is too small, there's nothing to eat, I can't kill anything fresh because all I have are pistols, and nothing's out this time of year anyhow."

"Let's get that bandage changed."

Hugh glowered at her. "I'm sure that will help me feel much better."

Edna narrowed her eyes at him. She hadn't missed the sarcasm in his voice.

"I'm sorry." He had a sudden understanding for Lachlan and the frustration that came with being incapacitated.

She made her way over and stopped, her hands hovering near his shirt. Bright spots of pink colored her cheeks. "Can I help you remove your shirt?"

With his good hand, he untucked the material, and she helped him slip it over his head.

He laid on the bed, much the same as the night before. Hugh could vaguely remember her climbing into the bed with him as she held the fresh bandage in place on his back.

Edna kept her eyes on the bandage at his front, then lifted it to expose the wound. She grimaced. Dipping the rag in the warm water, she dabbed at the stitches and stared at his shoulder, chewing her lip. This close, he could see the shine of wetness as her lip slowly slid free of her teeth. "I don't know that I've done enough. Calendula isn't strong enough for a wound this big. We need something from the apothecary."

"We're a bit far from there."

She brushed away his quip. "How long will Pete be gone?"

"Hard to say. He might just be working the line for a few days."

"Or he could be visiting family for the holidays. That

would mean he'll be gone through New Year's." With a feather-light touch, she smeared more of the salve onto his wound.

Hugh shook his head. "Not Pete. Trap line, supplies, home. That's it for him."

"Doesn't he have any family?"

"He does."

Edna placed a fresh bandage over the stitches. Then she laid a strip of fabric over top. She leaned over him and he lifted so she could wind the fabric under his arm and out the top. She tugged it gently, then tied off the top. When she moved away, her hair brushed Hugh's face and he closed his eyes for the briefest second, pretending she was this close out of desire and not duty.

"Why are you so sure he isn't visiting them for the holiday?" She put the lid on the salve and dipped the old bandages in the warm water, swishing them with her fingers.

"I was friends with his son."

"Ah." She nodded. "Why are you so certain he won't be visiting his son for Christmas?"

"His son lies in the Dragonfly Creek Cemetery."

Her throat bobbed and her lips parted. She searched his eyes and finally said, "I'm sorry."

Hugh shrugged his good shoulder. "It was a few years back." But that didn't lessen the anger he still felt. Jimmy had worked himself into the ground, literally. He was desperate for extra furs, more every year. He'd extended his trap line, going deeper into the woods. It was a good year for beaver, so he'd gone out to the lake almost every day. Until the day that lake had claimed his life.

Edna touched his elbow. "You were good friends."

He met her eyes and knew it wasn't a question. She'd read his face.

He nodded and drew a deep breath. "Pete comes to Dragonfly Creek to visit the cemetery and buy a few supplies. I believe it's the only reason he stays this close to the road."

Edna gaped at him. "We're more than half a day's walk from the road."

Hugh nodded. "With a horse and wagon, it's nearly a full day. He sleeps on the ground, but he should be staying with us."

Hugh looked around the space. The bed was pushed against the wall. Why not when there was nobody to get in on the other side? The interior was dark and lonely. Hugh's throat tightened. How could Pete bear to live here, alone, with only his memories for company?

"He doesn't have any other children?"

He swallowed the sadness. "Not in Dragonfly Creek. His daughters are in Billings, and when you meet Pete, you'll understand why he would never live there."

Edna surveyed the space. Perhaps she already understood.

Hugh sat up. With his one good arm, he tried to pull his shirt back on, but it caught over his head. "He hates the city." He spoke through the material.

Edna's voice was closer now, and she tugged at his shirt. Instead of helping him into it, she pulled it off completely.

"Hey—" He started to object, but she put her arm through the sleeve and took his hand in hers. Then she slid the sleeve up his arm and over his shoulder. Once it was over his head, he slipped his good arm in and his shirt fell to his waist. "That was quite fancy, Ms. Archer."

She turned, gathering the medicines, and walked to the cupboard. "I had plenty of time last night to contemplate how to get you back into a shirt."

Hugh's ears burned. "I don't remember much." He considered for the smallest moment adding that he hadn't yet forgotten waking up with her at his side, but thought better of it. He was, after all, at the mercy of her medical touch.

"So Pete doesn't ever see his other children? That's a bit harsh, don't you think?"

Hugh conceded that it might be. "Who am I to judge? Only he knows his reasons."

"Reasons for abandoning family." She placed her hands on her hips and pinned Hugh with a stare. "You're one of the most devoted men I know. You can't tell me you understand a man abandoning his family."

"It's not as though they need him. They're grown with families of their own. And…"

"What?" Her voice was as unforgiving as a winter in this forest, and Hugh regretted his words.

"It's just…Pete's been through a lot. I suppose he has good reason for isolating himself." Hugh looked around the space. So dark and dreary, even during the day. Why hadn't the man put in more windows and a reasonable stove? It was as though he took pleasure in the discomfort and grimness of his cabin.

"There are enough people in the world without a pa. It's a pity for a man to mock that."

"He's not mocking anything. It's not about them. It's about him."

Edna walked to the drying rack and lifted Hugh's coat. A hole had been torn through the shoulder, surrounded by the dark stain of his blood, but it wasn't anything he couldn't patch. She felt around the seams and, with a satisfied nod, she folded it and set it on Pete's shelf. He almost laughed at how at home she already was.

"Sounds selfish to me."

"It's not selfish. He lost his boy, and he blames society. I do too."

"Well, was his son lynched by the town?"

"How wild do you think the West still is?"

Edna gave a soft laugh. "I'm only saying Jimmy's death wasn't anyone's fault."

Hugh swallowed. Hearing her say Jimmy's name was surprisingly painful. Even worse was the thought that Edna and anyone else who moved to town would know Jimmy by name only. It made his loss feel all the more present.

"His wife worked him to the ground."

"I think you're giving the wife a bit too much credit."

"Am I?" Hugh heard the edge to his voice, but he wanted her to argue. The pain in his heart would be easier to bear if it was anger instead of sadness.

She shrugged. "Maybe you're not. I guess I don't know."

Hugh waited, still ready for a fight, but she didn't give it to him. He couldn't even look at her. "I suppose *you* don't care much about what society thinks."

Edna tilted her head and her brows pulled together. "What do you mean?"

"I mean you shared my bed last night."

Even in the dim cabin he could see color flood her cheeks. "I didn't...you were injured and you'd drank plenty..."

"D'you think a drunk man is safer than a sober one?"

"I guess not, but—"

"We can never tell anyone."

She jutted her chin in the air. "I didn't intend to."

"You trust me to be discreet?"

"Yes," She laughed, but it sounded fabricated, like she was an actress on a stage. "You're...Hugh."

"And that means..."

"It means you're Fay's brother, you're—"

"I'm not *your* brother."

Edna scoffed. "I know *that*."

"But you don't care what society thinks."

"I do."

"Do you not plan to stick around long enough to suffer the consequences?" Perhaps that was why she was hesitant to go home. She knew she wouldn't be coming back.

When her eyes flashed with anger, Hugh knew he'd pushed her too far. She yanked her stockings from the drying rack, running her hand down the length and hanging them once again. "I don't know why you're so upset. Your precious Catherine won't know anything. You were incapacitated last night, too drunk to do anything but fall to the floor. You were injured, and I had no intention of sleeping on the floor. It's a ridiculous rule, for we are able to do anything inappropriate at any time of the day. I don't see what's so special about darkness."

Precious Catherine. Her words echoed in his head. Fay's words after the dance joined the echo, and together they swirled a waltz in his mind. A tangle of limbs and emotions that even Hugh couldn't solve. He stood and roughly tucked his shirt into his pants. "I'm going to see what there is to do outside."

Rather than wait for her assistance, he flung his coat over his shoulders and stepped outside. He drew a deep breath of the crisp air, letting the cold freeze his anger. He wasn't even angry with Edna. He was angry with himself. Why was Catherine waiting for him? Everyone in town expected him to marry her, yet Catherine should have been doing her best to set them right. He'd been frank with her and had earned himself a slap to the face in the process. Over time though, she'd warmed up to him again, and they had become friends once more. Except he couldn't deny that he'd recently realized her feelings for him were more than friendly. If her expectations had ever been corrected, they were off course again.

To be any clearer, he would have had to ignore her

completely. Perhaps that was what he should do, avoid all social events until she married. Maybe it was his responsibility to avoid events in town unless he intended to marry. He was stuck in an in-between. A young, single male, but also one not ready or willing to shackle a woman to a life like his. He should be looked at like an adolescent, too young and poor to be considered a proper marriage candidate. He'd surely acted like an adolescent just now with Edna.

He didn't dare go back inside, not until he was sure he wouldn't try to pick a fight with the one woman he wanted shackled to him.

11

EDNA HELD the tiny iron key in her palm. After Hugh had stormed out, she'd done a more thorough search of the cabin and found it in the toe of an old boot. She might have worn the boots herself if they'd not been several sizes too big.

She exited the cabin, letting the door clang shut to announce her appearance. She didn't know if she'd encounter ornery Hugh again. A small smile teased at the corner of her mouth. Never had she seen Hugh be anything but even-tempered. His outburst was far gentler than anything she'd seen from Brandon. And yet it had been bad enough in Hugh's eyes to step away.

She wondered about Hugh's friend, and how society really had played into his death. Unless Pete was a glutton for punishment, why else would he exile himself so thoroughly? Why else would he refuse his family love? But love was a two-way street. Why had none of his living children come to him for the holidays?

She heard a whistled tune, the same one he'd entertained her with in the coach, before the rain came and drowned out the song. As she stepped off the porch, she found Hugh at the spring that ran into the creek. He squatted low as he lined the edge with rocks to make a sort of wall where the water ran off. She cleared her throat, and he stopped whistling his song and turned, his bad arm tucked into his stomach. He wore an expression of curiosity, but no hint of anger.

"What was that song?"

Hugh shrugged. "Just something to occupy my mind."

The tune didn't sound like the type to be made up off-hand. She considered his profile as he worked placing rocks along the shore, wondering why he was pretending. Edna held out her hand and opened it to show the key in her palm.

He wiped his wet hand on his pants and came closer. "The key. Where did you find it?" He plucked it from her hand, and it looked like a child's toy between his fingers.

Edna shrugged. "It was in an old boot. I haven't tried it. It might not even work."

Hugh smirked and offered her an arm. "Shall we take a look?" She took his arm and they strode to the root cellar once more.

Soon the lock was off and Hugh pulled the door open, making a groove in the freshly fallen snow. Inside were two long walls lined with shelves. At the back were shovels and other tools Edna knew little about.

Hugh stepped right in and gathered glass jars of pears and tomatoes. Edna felt in her belly that same twang of guilt she'd had when he opened Pete's home for the first time. Could they really just eat his stores?

Hugh passed a jar to Edna, and she took it with a tenta-tive hand. Hugh laughed, and she met his eyes, which shone with humor and affection. "We'll replace what we take."

Edna nodded, but only accepted what Hugh passed to her. He knew Pete well enough to use his hospitality. But Edna remained a stranger, a troublemaker, and they hadn't yet gotten away with any of this. She still harbored a fear that

Pete would turn up at any moment, pointing a rifle and demanding answers.

When Hugh was satisfied, they stepped out, and he shut and locked the door once more.

Edna adjusted the jars in her arms. "What happens if there's been a heavy snowfall and he can't get the door open?"

Hugh glanced at the track the door had made in the snow. "This way, the door is resting against the frame. It's stronger against both snow and anything else that might like to bust inside."

The thought of something wanting into that cellar sent a chill up the back of Edna's neck. "That's why he has the beams across his cabin door. Because it opens the wrong way?"

Hugh led the way back to the house. "I don't know that it is the 'wrong' way. He won't be in the root cellar long enough to get snowed in, so he doesn't have to be worried about that." He glanced about the forest, gaze lighting on the snow-heavy branches and the powdery white surrounding their shoes. "Snow can fall heavily overnight. If his cabin's door closed like the cellar door does, he might be stuck."

"But he has a covered deck." They entered the cabin and set their goods on the tabletop.

"He didn't always." Hugh chewed the inside of his cheek, and his eyes got a faraway look. "I think he built the deck four or so years ago."

Hugh took the pot off the stove and poured the warm water into a large bowl. "If you'll wash those potatoes, I'll get us more water."

He returned and they worked together, making a meal of sliced potatoes covered with crushed tomatoes and juice with dried basil. Hugh punctuated their work with the occasional hum of that same song he'd been whistling earlier. The tune, whatever it was, had lodged in his head, and Edna smiled. Her mama often hummed at the bakery. The familiarity of working alongside someone in the kitchen made Edna feel like she was home. It wasn't this cabin that did it. It was Hugh who made her feel so. She'd grown so accustomed to him these last few months. Perhaps home was a person, not a place.

She glanced at him, surprised at how well he knew his way around a kitchen. She'd never seen him in one. Mrs. Morris was like any other woman out west—eternally in the kitchen preparing, cooking, cleaning. There was always something to be done. But Hugh was a man. His job resided elsewhere, and yet he'd concocted a meal from Pete's supplies as though it was merely a different animal to skin.

Once they'd placed the dish in the small oven compartment on the side of the stove, Edna looked around. The sun was already beginning to set. She'd grown warm while working in the kitchen, but the cabin still held a chill sharp enough to warrant her staying near the stove.

Hugh called her over and gestured to the chair. In front of it, on the table, sat a bowl of pears.

Edna glanced at Hugh. "We can't eat them plain. They're too precious. Let me make a sweet loaf."

Hugh shook his head. "Just enjoy it."

She sat down while Hugh scooped up his own bowl of pears. He dug in first, so Edna figured she may as well indulge. The fruit was like manna on her tongue, as sweet and perfect as a fresh pear bought at market.

Hugh tipped his bowl back, drinking the juice. Edna laughed and did the same. Even the syrup tasted sugary sweet.

She licked her lips as Hugh took her empty bowl, swished the dishes in a pot of water, and dried them.

"I'd never have thought being stuck in the wild like this would be so relaxing. You'll spoil me for good, Mr. Morris."

Hugh grimaced. "My pa is Mr. Morris."

Edna laughed. "Do you prefer I call you Cowboy?"

"Much." He had a twinkle in his eye that made Edna's stomach twirl like a little child in a new dress. She smiled to herself, but the light expression didn't last long. For this was how it had started with Brandon. Easy, friendly. It hadn't been until he loved her, romantically, that he'd turned possessive and angry.

She watched Hugh as he pulled the dish from the oven. How could Hugh watch Catherine at the dances and allow other men to spin her on the dance floor? Did he not care for Catherine the way Brandon had cared for Edna? Or was Hugh simply a different sort of man? The kind who didn't care whether he was the favorite. Who had enough self-respect to walk away when he sensed a woman wasn't interested.

Hugh dished each of them a serving and set the plates on the table. "If you'll help me pull the table over, I'll sit on the bed for my seat."

They did so, though Edna offered little help lifting the heavy object.

Hugh smirked. "I fear you've lost your strength."

Edna laughed. "I can't deny you're right. It's unsettling, especially because I don't know how to get it back. Who'd have thought the work at Aster Ridge would be easier than in Chicago?"

They sat to eat, Edna in the one chair and Hugh on the edge of the bed. After the first bite, Edna groaned with pleasure. "*So much* better than plain pancakes."

Hugh chuckled. "I thought you were trying to poison me last night."

Edna gave his arm a playful push. "Nobody told me there

was an entire store down the path." She looked around. "Why does Pete only have one chair? Didn't you say he had this cabin when his wife was still alive?"

Hugh nodded. "There used to be four. I don't know where the others went. Mrs. Corbin, his wife, didn't come up here often. But he and Jimmy did." He grew quiet and his throat bobbed. "I always thought he moved out here to feel closer to Jimmy. But…" He shook his head.

Edna waited, wanting him to finish. The air in the cabin felt charged with whatever revelation Hugh was holding onto, but he just tucked into his meal once more.

After they'd cleaned up the dishes and covered the leftovers, Hugh set to work laying out his blankets.

Edna watched with a buttoned lip. He might not have gotten as angry as Brandon, but she'd still never seen that pained side of Hugh before. She wasn't keen to bring up the subject that had made his hurt rear its ugly little head. During her search of Pete's cabin earlier, she'd not found any more blankets. It seemed foolish to only keep as many blankets as he needed. Edna longed to move the bed closer to the stove, but it was made of solid wood and she didn't dare ask Hugh to help her move it. She was certain he'd accept, no matter how it might pain him. Instead, she stood as close to the fire as she could, warming her clothes, before climbing into bed.

Rather than replace Pete's potatoes, Edna vowed she would replace his stove with a larger one. The man might want to avoid society, but he didn't need to suffer while he did so.

No doubt she and Hugh would both suffer tonight, sleeping without the other's body heat. She wasn't sure when he'd moved to the floor, but it must have been late enough in the morning that she'd not grown chilly without him near.

Perhaps he was right, and she did flaunt the standards of

society. Try as she might, she couldn't force herself to care. Especially not as she tucked herself between chilled sheets.

IN THE MORNING, Edna woke from what had possibly been the worst night's sleep she'd ever experienced. No matter how tightly she'd curled, her body refused to lend enough heat to allow her comfort and rest. Several times, she'd considered joining Hugh on the ground since he refused to join her in the bed. She barely stopped herself glaring at Hugh's serene, sleeping face as she dressed. She tugged Pete's chair over to the stove and sat with her knees practically touching it, begging for its warmth to move through her body.

Fresh snow had fallen in the night and coated the edges of the windows. With each snowfall, they were less likely to leave, and Pete less likely to arrive. Would they be here all winter? A bleak thought if last night was any indication of what she could expect. She warmed her hands and promised herself she would find any excuse to not sleep in that bed alone ever again.

Hugh was awake and putting away his bed when Edna asked, "What was that word you used? The thing you said we would get if we slept outside? Chilblains?"

Hugh nodded. "Some people call it frostbite. It's when you lose a part of yourself to the cold."

"Like a toe?" Edna had heard of frostbite. Frederick's pa had treated a case when they were young. Frederick had told Brandon and Edna how the man's toe was black, not purple like a bruise, but black like a rogue sheep's wool.

"A toe if you're lucky. I've seen pockmarked faces from chilblains, and even a man who lost a nose."

"A nose." Edna touched the cold tip of her own. A gruesome image to be sure. She couldn't decide which was worse, for the nose to be black, or to be gone altogether.

"I'm glad you saw sense and decided to sleep in here."

Edna glowered at him, but he was too busy setting the blankets on the shelf to notice. It might be warmer inside, but last night had been anything but comfortable—and it wasn't only due to the man who had been breathing deeply on the floor, taunting her with the warmth she knew he held. This wasn't a new sensation. For Hugh had been warmth long before they'd come to this snowy forest. Her admiration for him had always beat in her chest, a glowing ember that refused to die, no matter how long it went without kindling. Just as now, he had ideas that were different from hers. The most prominent one being which woman he would marry, if he ever got the chance. Edna was certain nothing that happened out here could induce him to change his mind on that matter. If Catherine couldn't convince him to marry, who was Edna to accomplish such a feat?

12

EDNA TIED off the handkerchief holding his bandages in place. To her immense relief the wound had actually looked better than this morning. It was still sticky and red, but less angry looking. Also, Hugh had yet to break a fever. She would pray it never came.

He moved to his bed on the floor and Edna forced herself to turn away from him and climb into her own bed. She pulled the blankets tight under her chin. If possible, the cold sliced sharper through her skin tonight than it had the night before. She'd been unable to summon the courage to demand he join her in bed. It seemed an entirely too lustful request to make, and every time she considered it, her tongue felt too large for her mouth.

When she closed her eyes, she pictured the roaring fireplace in the Grahams' home. She could almost feel the warmth that would heat her hands as she held them out. Not too hot, but nearly there. Even the cushions she would sit on would be warmed by the flames, heating the half of her that wasn't facing the fire.

Instead, she was stuck in this frigid cabin with a too-small stove that never heated the entire space no matter how much wood Edna stuffed into it.

And they were eating through the wood so quickly, Edna knew she'd soon need to chop more. Hugh wouldn't be able to help, not with a hole through his shoulder.

Hole or not, the ripped muscle and the expanse of exposed chest attached to it was still hard and strong, solid and reliable. She blew frustration through her lips at how little control she still had, even after months of work. She considered her rule to never fall for a man who elicited emotions. At this rate, she would be an old maid before she allowed herself to take interest in a man. Perhaps, with such a bleak future ahead of her, she should have touched him more while tending him. Instead of a clinical touch, she might have noticed him with a woman's appreciation instead.

Hugh's rumbling voice came from the ground. "You still awake?"

"Yes." *And thinking about most inappropriate things.* "Do you need anything?" She hoped he did, if only for the distraction.

"Just a bit of chatter to calm my mind. If you're up to it."

Edna smiled. This was the most demanding he'd been since they arrived. She was happy to oblige. "Chatter? Too bad Fay isn't here."

A snort came from below. "I'd be dead by now if she was tending me. That girl has all the tenderness of a grizzly."

Edna laughed and shifted, then moved back to her original spot. A bit of warmth had already bled into the sheets, and she wasn't about to let it go to waste.

Hugh said, "There's a game Lachlan and I would play when we couldn't sleep."

Edna realized they must have shared a bed. Was their family so poor that even their youngest brother, Otto, had shared it too? How did they ever sleep with three brothers in a single bed? Certainly they slept warm, warmer than Edna was now. She wouldn't mind a warm body beside her, helping remove the chill from the sheets. "What game?" It would have to be a quiet game, else they would have woken their parents.

"Challenge or Truth."

Edna turned to her side, abandoning the little warmth in favor of looking at Hugh as he taught her this game. It was a pointless action, for she couldn't see him in the dark. Surrounded by all these trees, barely a streak of moonlight made its way in the small cabin windows. Or perhaps it was the clouds that had released snow the entire day, blocking the moon from view. "Teach me."

"One person asks another whether they'd like to tell a truth or accept a challenge. Then the next person gets a turn."

"Tell a truth?" Edna chuckled. "That should be easy. Did you always choose that one?"

"Not when we had something to hide."

Edna's stomach turned.

"You ready?" Hugh asked. His voice was different, as though he'd turned on his side too.

"Are you lying on your arm?" The stitches would bust, and Edna would be forced to sew him up again. At the idea, something fluttered in her chest, and she wasn't sure if it was apprehension or excitement.

"I'm on my back. Truth or Challenge, Edna Archer."

A laugh hummed up in her throat. "Challenge."

"Okay." Hugh drew out the word, like he needed to think of his next move.

When Edna blinked, the space was so dark that closing her eyelids did almost nothing to change the scene. She chewed her lip, considering what type of thing she would challenge someone. Maybe to lift something heavy, but she couldn't ask that of Hugh, not with his shoulder. Perhaps she would ask him to drink a full cup of coffee, but that was a waste of supplies, and he needed his sleep. She imagined he already got too little sleep on the floor.

"Get a log for the fire," Hugh finally said.

Edna laughed. An easy enough task, though she doubted it would fit in the stove. She'd stuffed it full before climbing into bed.

She slid out, keeping the blankets closed to preserve some of the warmth she'd generated. She padded on stockinged feet over to the metal bucket that held the wood.

"Not from in here. From the woodpile."

Edna's hand froze. She turned slowly to Hugh. "You want me to go out into the snow and get a wet piece of wood to put on the fire?"

When he spoke again, she could hear the smile in his voice. "You don't have to put it on right away. But it will be used for the fire eventually."

Edna twisted her mouth. So *this* was what the challenges were. They weren't a test of strength or useful in any way. They were arbitrary and would mean not only the heat in the bed would be gone, but her skin would be chilled as well. But she wasn't about to lose this game. She'd decided which challenge she would give to Hugh, and she meant to deliver it.

Edna straightened and pulled her shawl from the hook by the door, wrapping it around her shoulders. Rather than button herself into her shoes, she stepped into Hugh's too-large boots, her stockinged feet finding the smooth spots where his toes rested, and slid the door latch. Once opened, she had to remove the cross beams all while the cold bit at her face and legs.

Once she'd cleared the doorway, she ran as fast as Hugh's boots would carry her, plucked a split log from the pile, and ran back to the cabin. It took longer to stir a spoonful of sugar into a cup of coffee, but her teeth were chattering by the time she'd replaced the bars and latched the door.

She dropped the log by Hugh's feet, glowering down at him. She was fairly certain she hated this game.

Hugh laughed. "Well done, Miss Archer. Well done."

Edna walked back to the spot along the wall and returned Hugh's boots to their resting place alongside hers. She kept her shawl on as she climbed back into the cold bed. "Are you ready for your challenge?"

"Challenge? I haven't told you yet whether I choose truth."

Edna froze. "But *I* chose challenge."

Hugh chuckled again. "All right. Challenge it is. What have you got?"

Edna moved her legs around, unable to find any semblance of warmth from before. "Get in here and warm this bed up for me."

There. She'd said it.

She'd wondered if she would be bold enough. But the shivering in her bones had granted her the courage—or perhaps the desperation— she hadn't had before he'd challenged her.

The familiar cadence of Hugh's breathing stopped. He lay completely still. No hint of laughter or of accepting her offer. Her cheeks heated, the only part of her that was warm at the moment. Why had she requested it? She wanted to take it back, to laugh now and pretend she had meant it as a joke. But she couldn't. Her challenge sat squat between them, a living, breathing thing with teeth.

"It's ridiculous for you to sleep on the floor with your injury. You don't need a game to help you fall asleep. You need a comfortable bed beneath you."

He still didn't move, and Edna wished she could convince herself that he'd fallen asleep. But the air of the entire cabin felt charged, like it had just been struck by lightning. He was awake, processing her words, and either had been struck dumb or didn't know how to deny her.

"Hugh, don't be silly. I know you well enough to know you won't do anything uncouth. I just want you to sleep, and I want a bit of your warmth. There's nobody here to be scandalized at our being alone or to claim anything happened that didn't happen. So will you drop this stubborn act and bring those blankets with you?" She bit her lips together, forcing herself to stop rambling.

He sighed, and Edna waited to see if the sound signaled refusal or acceptance. The blankets rustled, and she felt glad for the darkness, as it hid the huge smile stretching across her face.

HUGH SHOOK his head the entire time he gathered his blankets. This was a bad idea. He'd been a model of self-control these past two days, letting Edna touch him and tend to him without reaching out and pulling her close. Now she was asking him to be closer, and who was he to refuse? He dropped his ball of quilts onto the bed and drew a slow breath. Edna climbed out of the bed, and this close he could make out the white of her shift below the darkness of her shawl. She must have kept it on after her foray outside.

Though his stomach performed cartwheels, he couldn't help but smile at how she'd barely paused before performing the challenge. He and his brothers had always grumbled and tried to get out of whatever challenge had been extended by offering up an easier challenge disguised as something harder.

Together they spread the quilts out on top of one another. If Edna hadn't suggested this, they likely both would have been chilled to the bone all night, just as he had been the night before. Pete didn't own four quilts so he and a guest could each have two. He owned four because there were nights when all were needed. Tonight was one of those nights. Hugh wished for a mercury temperature gauge to see just how cold it was. But it didn't matter.

Edna tucked herself back in, unusually silent. After extending such a dare, she should be gloating or doing something to make Hugh feel conquered. She'd never played the game, though, and he tried to convince himself that was why she kept her silence now. It wasn't that she regretted her choice or worried about Hugh sleeping so near.

Feeling blindly, he pulled back all but one of the quilts and climbed inside. He almost groaned in pleasure at the softness of the bed. He'd not expected Pete to have more than a single buffalo hide to cushion the rails, but this mattress was feather, a rare luxury, and after two nights on the floor with a hole in his shoulder, this felt like a cloud. He shifted deeper into the blankets and noticed Edna lay as still as a stuffed bear.

"This might be the easiest challenge I've ever received. It's certainly more comfortable than running to the wood pile."

"I'll think of a better one for next time." The silence stretched, and she spoke again. "What was the worst challenge you ever did?"

Hugh chuckled. "You think I'm going to give you ideas?" He rubbed his icy feet together, but already he was warmer than he'd been on the floor. Her suggestion to share the bed was practical only. Edna wasn't fond of him in any way other than Fay's helpful older brother. But he hadn't imagined the way her gaze lingered on his bare chest, or the way she bit her lip after she'd caught herself and turned away. "Truth or Challenge?"

"Why do you always get to go first?"

"Because it was my idea. Choose." Only the smallest shred of guilt waved its tiny hand at how Hugh took advantage of Edna being new to the game.

"Truth. It's too cold for any more of your challenges." She shivered as though the mere memory chilled her.

Hugh grinned. Being this close to her, even though she was under one more quilt than he, certainly offered a distraction. She might have thought he'd sleep better for not feeling his injury against the floor, but her proximity kept his mind off the pulsing, radiating pain better than a thousand feather mattresses.

He considered what truth he would ask for. Should he call her out for gawking at him while she was supposed to be tending him? No, he wanted her to look more. To see more of him away from Fay. To see him as a man instead of a fill-in brother.

Then he remembered why they were in this predicament in the first place. "Why didn't you want to go home for Christmas?"

She didn't gasp, but her breathing stopped, and this close, it had the same effect. He had hit on the greatest reward of this game, hitting on a secret.

"W-what do you mean?"

Her stammer said everything. He wished it weren't so dark. Once again, he was denied the chance to decipher her facial reaction to the question of Christmas at home.

She cleared her voice. Perhaps she, too, heard the desperation it contained, the truth it told. "Of course I want to go home. To see my mother."

"I think Willem took away your reasons not to go, and you had no other choice. Heaven knows you took long enough to leave. Long enough that Lachlan had a spell and I didn't have a companion up on that seat."

The scratch of fabric told him Edna had turned her head. "You're saying it's my fault we're stuck here?"

Hugh thought for a second. "You didn't try to rob us of our coach, or hold a gun to my belly."

"But you're saying if I hadn't left the leaving to so late, you would have had a companion. And what? Lachlan would have shot and killed those three men?"

Hugh could imagine the scene. "More likely Lachlan would have shot *at* them, and they would have turned tail and run away like the cowards they are."

Edna didn't answer. She shifted and turned her back to Hugh, and when she spoke, her voice sounded far away. "I didn't mean for any of this to happen. I'm sorry you have to spend Christmas here in this cold cabin with a woman you hardly know."

Hugh's chest tightened. He hadn't meant any of that. His prying words about Christmas weighed on him, slowed his breathing. He probably would have been better off teasing her for gawping at his bare chest. She would have been embarrassed, but not angry with him.

"That's not what I meant. I'll ask something else—"

Edna rolled onto her back once more and cut him off. "No. You asked, and I answered. Your turn. Truth or challenge?"

13

HUGH CROSSED his ankles and counted Edna's breaths as he considered her question. *Truth or challenge.* She was moving on from his question, but he wasn't quite ready. Either he wanted more of an answer, or he wanted to apologize for making her feel like he blamed her in any way. He didn't blame her. He only wanted to know what had caused her to wait so long. She hadn't answered, not really, but Hugh wasn't of mind to press her further.

Finally, Hugh drew a breath. "Truth."

"Why haven't you married Catherine Price?"

His breath froze in his lungs. Possibly it was literally frozen, because the air in the cabin hurt to breathe.

"I think Fay has spun you a story."

"No, she hasn't. Anyone with eyes knows Catherine is sweet on you. She expects you to secure her hand any day."

Secure her hand. He wasn't capable of securing anything for anyone, not even himself.

Edna continued. "She's rather pretty, and her family is respectable. I do wonder, though, if something happened between her younger sister and Fay…"

Edna fell silent and Hugh knew he'd run out of time to answer. "I guess I don't love her."

"Don't love her? But you spend your time with her."

"I don't spend my time with her. I spend my time at our farm, working."

"Okay, well, you spend the dances with her on your arm."

Hugh turned his face to Edna. Had he heard a thread of jealousy? Did Edna want him to spend the dances with *her*?

He shook away the fantasy. Edna knew too much about his family's circumstances to consider him for a romance. It was a wonder Catherine even allowed his attentions. No woman with options would choose Hugh.

"I do spend the dances with her. Perhaps I shouldn't." Fay had told him as much numerous times. "But she's a lot of fun. She's always telling a story or making everyone laugh. She's easy to be around."

"But you don't love her."

"I can't make her happy."

Edna rolled over to face him, and two forces inside him clashed swords. He both wanted to shift away and to pull her to him. If he hadn't been wounded, the side that wanted her closer would most definitely have won out. As it stood, he was in no state to be pulling anyone anywhere.

"I dare say," Edna said, her tone tentative as a tiptoe, "she'd be rather delighted to marry you."

"Possibly. For a time. But she's…" Hugh stopped, unwilling to reveal this side of Catherine. He doubted many people had spent enough time in her presence to notice, and then time out of her presence to be released from her charm enough to recognize it for what it was. She was the type of person who talked about others. She was always telling a story—about someone. How they'd done something so foolish, or selfish, or if they hadn't done something negative, how they'd done something good, but it was completely out of character for them.

After a time, Hugh began to wonder what she said about him when he wasn't around. Or worse, what she said about his family. He would never attach himself to someone like that. She was a smiling, good timing, laughing poison.

"What is she?" Edna pressed.

He closed his mind to Catherine's flaws. They didn't matter so much as his own. "I couldn't make any woman happy, least of all one who has grown up with everything."

"Don't be so self-deprecating. Catherine isn't the only woman in town who would like to marry you. I only wonder which of the others would be brave enough to cross her."

Hugh smiled, knowing the gesture was hidden in the inky black that surrounded them. "Again, Fay has told you too much. She thinks the same, but you are both wrong. Women want a man who can provide. I'm too busy providing elsewhere. I could not provide for a wife." His smile had faded. Why had he told Edna all that? There was only one reason to spell it out for her, and it must be because he had lost all hope of her ever loving him.

"Please, tell me more about what women want. I'm glad to have met someone with so much *knowledge*." Her voice was thick with sarcasm.

Hugh laughed. "You tease, but I know the basics. It's the reason Eloise married Aaron. Our family knows love is not enough. Unfortunately, love alone cannot pay the mortgage or put food in the crock, elsewise we'd be doing just fine."

Edna's voice was quiet. If he weren't lying inches away from her, he would not have heard. "Love isn't money. If you had to work for it, it wouldn't be love."

EDNA LAY next to Hugh with the quilt tucked around her chin and her fingers interlaced over her stomach. "So, you'll never, ever marry? Not Catherine, not anyone?"

"Maybe one day."

"You sound doubtful."

Hugh drew a slow breath, the air moving past his lips in a way she could hear in this silent cabin. "I don't know, but I've answered many of your questions. Truth or challenge?"

Edna gave a soft laugh. He'd given her far more than she gave him, and she wouldn't begrudge him the change of topic. "Truth." Was there really any other answer to this game?

"Why do you avoid the men who are interested in you, romantically?"

"I don't avoid anyone."

"Truth." Hugh warned.

Edna picked at her nails under the covers. "I left someone behind."

"You're promised?"

"No, but I didn't like how I felt about him. Like I couldn't live without him. I'm not ready to wrestle with those feelings again."

"But you've learned how…to live without him." It wasn't a question, but a confirmation.

Edna nodded. "But he's still in my memory." Silence. She wondered vaguely what Hugh was thinking, but as usual, when Brandon broke into her mind, little else penetrated. He'd always taken up too much space. "I decided I would never give my affection to another man unless he didn't stir anything inside me."

Hugh laughed. *Laughed.* The sound punched at Edna's heart, which was already swollen at talk of Brandon and what she'd allowed to happen to her in Chicago. She'd fallen in love with a man who didn't love her in return. Perhaps he thought he loved her, but Brandon's love had been conditional, and more often than not, Edna hadn't met his requirements. She'd experienced little else to match that pain.

But Hugh's laugh hurt, too. "You find my troubles entertaining?"

He reached over and touched her hip with his hand. "Not your troubles, but your vow. If you ignore any man who stirs something, then you've limited yourself to never being in love."

"You said it yourself. Love isn't the answer."

"Well... I... That's not what I meant."

"Isn't it? Love isn't convenient for you. Well, it isn't for me either."

"I never said it wasn't *convenient* for me. It's just that I can't build a home with love. I can't feed a family with love. You, you don't have to worry about all of that."

"Don't I? You say you won't marry because you're not rich enough. But you would fault a woman for choosing a man who *is* rich enough to marry." Any man would be bitter at the idea of being judged on his money rather than himself. Same way a woman wants to be seen for more than her beauty.

"I would not fault her." The flatness of his voice, with no hint of defensiveness, told her everything. He spoke true.

"Would you fault a woman for wanting to marry you without wealth?"

Hugh huffed as though her suggestion was ridiculous. But she'd heard his feelings about Catherine and they didn't make sense. He enjoyed her presence and no doubt found her beautiful. What else was there?

But the moment she had the thought, she remembered Brandon. He had been much the same. Handsome, wealthy even, a future lay before him. And charismatic. Everyone loved him. Edna had been lucky to be the woman he chose.

Except she didn't always feel lucky when they were alone. She felt like a dog, kicked and cowering.

His expectations were too high. Once she'd learned to rise to the bar he held, he would have been happy with her. Instead, she'd run away. She was certain he would never forgive her for what she'd done. But the thing was, she didn't care. Away from his charm, she finally felt free of him. Going home was the worry. Once she entered his sphere, she might fall under his spell once more, wanting to please him, wanting to prove herself worthy of his love.

Hugh's deep voice cut into her fearful musings. "I would not fault her for it, but I also would not accept it. She might not understand what poor is like." He swallowed. "I do."

"And if she's willing to live in it for love of you?"

Hugh took a moment before answering. "Perhaps your way of thinking isn't entirely wrong. Perhaps we should all enter marriage with calculation rather than passion."

Her heart shrank away from his words. She recognized his words were a mirror of her own, but those words from Hugh's mouth sharpened to a knife point and lodged in her gut. He deserved passion. Everyone did. A small voice in her mind asked, *except for you?* But she'd had her turn with passion in those early days with Brandon. When their friendship had turned into more. Before Brandon had morphed into someone else.

"What if the girl who wanted to marry you was an orphan, starving for food and family? You would be rescuing her."

"Why couldn't she get anyone better than me?"

"She's homely and skinny," Edna answered quickly.

Hugh laughed and Edna felt the vibration through the bed. She blushed. They were so very close, and him sober. How would they both feel about this come morning?

"Okay, I might consider the homely girl if she needed me. My poor house might not be so measly to her."

"You might still struggle to feed your family. All those same trials would be there. They would just be endured with a different set of expectations."

"I suppose expectations are my issue with Catherine. Nobody lives up to her expectations. Ever. I surely wouldn't be the exception."

Edna chewed her cheek, unsure whether she should tell him her mind. Was it her place to resolve the confusion with Catherine—to tell him he should let her go? Edna knew better than most that letting someone go wasn't easy. For Hugh's sake, she hoped that Catherine living in town meant Hugh wouldn't have to watch the woman he loved court and marry another. He may not want to saddle her with him for fear of being a disappointing husband, but that didn't mean he didn't still love and admire her, or that he wanted to watch her fall in love. Wanting someone to be different doesn't make stepping away any easier. It also doesn't mean love isn't present and beating just as powerfully as before.

More than helping him to let Catherine go, Edna wanted him to see his worth. To see that maybe Catherine wasn't the wife for him, but there was any number of women who would love nothing more than to sleep at his side, and not only for warmth's sake. Edna was certain, because she was one of them.

14

EDNA WOKE to find Hugh already awake and out of bed. She turned over and watched him as he looked out the window. There wasn't much to see. She knew because she'd stared out that tiny square often enough. She supposed Pete must not spend much time inside his cabin. His covered porch would be a fine resting place in the summer.

Hugh stared with such commitment that Edna rose, wrapping a blanket around her shoulders, and came to stand behind him.

"What are you looking at?"

Hugh jumped and turned. A wide smile stretched his face, and he laughed. "You have the feet of a hunter." He turned back. "They're wasted in the kitchen."

"Are you saying my baking skills are subpar?"

He laughed again. She wished she could bottle up the sound and listen to it whenever she pleased. He was freer here. Though his shoulder was hurt, it was somehow unburdened.

"I think Pete has the right of it out in these woods," she said, "Far away from the noise and the cruelty of the world."

Hugh turned to her with a raised brow. "You think it's not cruel out here? I suppose the bears that there door is boarded against are just like a snuggly child's toy?"

His words, though contradicting her, were anything but harsh. A smile lifted his lip, and his bright teeth showed with every word.

"If anyone could turn a bear into a stuffed toy, it would be you. Although if I was snuggling it at night, I think I might prefer a small rabbit to a large bear. Too many claws and teeth."

Hugh's smile was rueful, and Edna's gaze snagged on the scruff of hair that now dusted his chin, stopping just before it reached his smooth lips.

Edna dropped her gaze to her cold hands and remembered the muff she'd lost in the commotion of losing the coach. "I lost the fur you gave me. I'd like to buy another when we return." She wasn't going to see her mama for Christmas anymore, but she could still send the muff as a parcel.

"I'll hold you to it. I don't give them out often, and never more than once." He gave her a sly look.

Edna laughed. "I didn't want you to give it to me in the first place! Do you think I'd let you give me one again?"

"I'm not going to. So don't even ask."

Edna smiled and had the urge to lean into him, to rest her head on his good shoulder. Why was he so easy, so different from other men? Was it that he was Fay's brother? Did he feel like a brother to her? Having no siblings, she didn't know. But she did know she wasn't supposed to want to wrap her arms around a brother, nor to feel his lips against hers. That was strictly for men who were far removed from family.

Hugh dipped his head, catching her gaze. "I was teasing.

In fact, if we can get those traps down, we might be able to catch you a fur of your own."

Edna looked at the metal contraptions along the walls. "You mean these aren't meant as decor? I thought he was going for a dungeon aesthetic."

"Well, he might be, but I can figure most of them. The trick will be finding one you can handle yourself." He gestured to his shoulder. "I cannot set it for you just now."

Edna tossed her head. "You think because there are no other gentleman around that you can drop the pretense of chivalry?"

Hugh's jaw dropped. "Seeing as how I got this hole in my shoulder while trying to get *you* to safety, I think I've earned an excess of chivalry to get me through for a few days."

"Yes, well tackling me to the floor used a bit of that excess. You're just about out."

Hugh narrowed his eyes. "I think your feet are wasted in a bakery, but so is your tongue. It's too sharp. You should be helping Mr. Pine at the auction block."

He scanned the traps along the wall and pointed to the one with the smallest chain, though the circular shape at the end was large enough to make her cringe at the thought of its purpose. "Think you can get that down from the wall?"

"Yes," Edna replied, though she was not so certain as she sounded. Metal tended to be heavier than it looked. True, she'd hauled plenty of heavy things while working for her mother, but she'd lost a bit of her strength out here in Montana. The work for Willem and the others at Aster Ridge wasn't nearly as difficult as it had been in Chicago.

Edna pulled the chair over to the wall and set one foot on the seat. Hugh came over and held his good arm up, as though to support her. She glanced pointedly at his hand. "You're going to save my life with one good hand?"

Hugh clutched at his chest, as though he'd been shot through the heart. "You wound me." His eyes snapped open again and he pinned her with an intensity she'd never seen. "My one arm is as good or better than two arms from your soft Chicago boys."

Edna faced the wall again with a gulp. She muttered as she released the chain from where it was strung along several nails in the wall. "It's different here. I didn't have many men in Chicago." She hefted the trap off its nail and passed it down.

Hugh took the trap with his good hand, a smile on his face as though to prove he was as strong as he said. "So you only had a few men after you in Chicago. Is that why you left?" He piled the trap on the ground, each link of the chain tapping the floor with a resounding click.

Edna's gaze flashed to his. She swallowed, but her throat stuck to itself and she coughed instead. He offered a hand and she took it, climbing down from the chair. She couldn't meet his eye and focused instead on putting the chair back, as though it took all her attention to do so.

Finally, she found her words and faced him. "No, I left because Willem made us an offer only a fool would refuse." That much was true. He was paying her too much when she factored in meals and board. But, also, she'd been that fool when she considered refusing the offer. If her mama hadn't found the letter... Edna didn't want to think about what might have happened if she'd shown the letter to Brandon first.

Hugh's teasing tone of voice disappeared. "I know a bit about being unable to refuse the Grahams' pay. Perhaps you are right. Only a fool would refuse."

Edna turned to him. "I didn't mean to call you a fool. I don't think—"

Hugh held up a hand. "I'm not offended. I know you weren't talking about me."

Edna gave him a deadpan look. "Actually, I was talking about you the entire time."

Hugh's gaze snapped to her, and she gave him a wide grin. He laughed and shook his head. "Should I spread my arms and allow you a few jabs to my gut as well? Or would you like to set a trap?"

"Is taking jabs an *actual* option? It would be far warmer."

Hugh plucked her shoes from by the door and held them aloft. Then he turned them and looked at them with disgust. "You cannot keep wearing these. They're practically moldy."

Edna snatched them from his hands and turned them. In the morning light, they did look a mess. "They aren't meant for traipsing through the woods in the rain. They're city boots, meant for storefronts and cobblestones."

Hugh raised his brows. "Around here, we make shoes fit for any situation."

Edna toed a bit of chain on the floor. "Maybe we can catch me a new pair." Edna was only partially joking, for in her earlier search of the cabin, she'd found a pair of fur slippers that looked to be the warmest footwear this side of the Mississippi.

Before long they were outside, but this time the snow crunched beneath their feet instead of the mud squelching. In fact, when Edna looked behind them, she noticed a trail of dried mud as it fell from their shoes. She could use them to find her way back to the cabin, her own version of Hansel's breadcrumbs.

She looked around the dense woods. How alike these were to that same children's story. A few long strides brought her closer to Hugh and, damaged as he was, she felt a sight safer. Child-eating witches might not live here, but animals aplenty did, and not all of them had four legs. She glanced back toward the house, trying to see if their chimney smoke rose above the trees, but the canopy blocked her view.

"Do you think those men will look for us?" she asked.

Hugh shrugged. "They might. But if they've come out this way before, I'd bet Pete has scared 'em away from ever coming back."

"And you're still certain he won't shoot *you*?"

Hugh shook his head. "So long as he recognizes me."

Edna reached a finger out and flicked the tip of his chin. "I barely recognize you with these whiskers. A few days more and you'll look like a wild man."

Hugh rubbed at his beard, which whispered against his palm. "If I do, I suppose he'll think he's looking in a mirror."

Edna's stomach twisted at the thought of running into this wild man who lived so far out here all alone. "How long have you known Pete?"

"All my life. Pete and his wife were always close with my folks, and you know Jimmy and I were pals."

Pals. The word brought to mind two little boys running in a field. "You mean to say you weren't always a bearded wild man?"

Hugh laughed. "I was. It was quite a fright to my ma when I was born."

Edna laughed outright, then clapped a hand over her mouth. Such noise in the quiet of this forest felt like a sort of blasphemy.

Hugh brushed her hand away. "There's nobody to hear you."

Edna gulped at his brief touch. Perhaps she'd been wrong and sharing a bed, however innocently they'd behaved, did alter more than she imagined. *Bandits.* She reminded herself to focus on the dangers, and not on his hand brushing hers. "Nobody to hear me? What if those bandits are nearby?"

"They'd probably think it was some lost cow braying."

Edna shoved at his good arm. Lucky for him, his injury was on the other side.

"The worst your laughter could do is cause a bit of snow to fall from those branches."

Edna eyed the many branches above them, heavy with snow. She didn't want it all on her head. Reason enough to stay quiet. She tucked her shawl tighter around her face and stepped closer to Hugh. If she had the mind, she could link her arm through Hugh's and steal a bit of his warmth.

Too soon, he veered off the trail and they picked through the underbrush. No easy feat when one considered how the dead branches clung to her skirts like needy children.

Finally, he stopped at a small clearing and dropped the chain and trap with a loud clang. "Probably should have shown you back at the cabin." He tugged the chain taut and gestured to the nail at the end. "We'll pound this into the tree, then set the trap."

Edna looked around. "Which tree?"

He gestured vaguely behind her. "We'll try not to disturb the area where we place it, so we'll open it here and then transfer it."

Edna raised her brows at the heavy object. It possessed a set of jagged metal teeth. "I'm supposed to walk around with that thing in my hands?"

Hugh smirked. "That depends. Where am I on that chivalry scale?"

"Out. You used it all when you walked me through a cold forest without offering me your coat."

Hugh laughed. "You're more bundled than I am." He ran his gaze along the line of her shawl, which under normal circumstances might look like he was appreciating her face. But these circumstances weren't normal, and he had eyes only for one girl. Money only kept him away from Catherine. She held his eye and his heart, but because he would never be rich, he would never give her his hand. Edna imagined it would be a long while before Hugh's heart and his mind boarded the same boat down the river.

"Still, I think you'll have to be the one to place the trap."

He nodded and pointed to the trap. The more she looked at it in the daylight, the more frightening it became. "If you can use both hands to pry it open, I can set the pin. Just keep your fingers out of the teeth."

They were actually called *teeth*. She gulped and squatted by the contraption. Each side had a small metal lip for her fingers. She pried them apart, but they had barely separated when Edna feared them snapping back together and catching her nose in the process. She didn't intend to lose her nose. Not to frostbite, or this trap. She carefully closed the contraption and set it by her side. "Actually, I don't want to catch anything. Let's go sit by the fire and play your game." She'd rather be challenged to run barefoot to the woodpile than pinch her face in this thing.

Hugh laughed so loud it echoed through the trees and white flakes of snow fell from the trees. From their spot in the clearing, she could see it fall as though watching a snowstorm from the heavens. She stood and shook the flakes from her skirt. "I'll split a bit of wood instead. Maybe we can get the cabin a bit warmer."

Hugh lifted the trap from the ground, the chain jangling as he hefted it onto his good shoulder. "That cabin is too big to get any warmer with the size of stove Pete's got. I'm beginning to wonder whether Pete pulls that bed closer to the stove in the winter."

Edna walked backwards so she faced Hugh. "Please tell me we can do that. It'd be a sight warmer."

Hugh chuckled. "If we did, I could sleep on the floor again."

Edna scoffed. "If you did, you would counter the additional warmth. It's Christmas Eve. Consider it a gift."

Hugh mumbled, and his words were just audible. "A gift for you or me?"

Edna didn't answer, just turned back again so she didn't trip and fall. The last thing she needed was an injury of her own. She glanced at Hugh's injured arm, tucked obediently into his stomach. He seemed to be healing well enough. Shouldn't a person with such an injury be resting instead of hauling traps into the wilderness? He caught her eye and smiled. It wasn't rueful like the one he gave when he was ribbing her. Instead it was soft, and it held...something. She didn't dare name it, for once named, she would latch onto it.

She silently cursed herself for getting so close to Hugh. He was the last man in Montana she should latch onto, the only one who stirred anything for her. She shut the trap on those thoughts. She hadn't been snared, nor was she going to be. The trap hadn't been fully opened or set. She was still safe so long as she didn't open anything. There was nothing to be sorry for. Yet.

15

Hugh waited until Edna was distracted, pulling a chair over to the wall to hang the trap back up, before he slipped his hand inside the neck of his shirt and scratched at the bandage. The action was so satisfying, the pain hardly even registered.

Edna cleared her throat. "A little help, if you please, or would you rather continue ripping your stitches open?"

Hugh glanced at her, the chain at the ground next to the chair and her fists on her waist. "Just because you're taller than me on that chair doesn't mean you get to command me."

He lifted the chain and passed it to her. Hanging the trap back up proved more difficult than taking it down. He mirrored the action he'd done when she'd taken it down, holding his good arm as high as it would go in case her foot slipped off the seat. Her skirts hid her battered boots, but from the way she was stretching and teetering, he knew she was on her tiptoes.

"Just leave it. You're going to fall."

"I have it." She grunted. "Just a bit—" As she hooked a link of chain over the last nail, her boot slipped on the seat of the chair and she fell against the wall. The shift in weight caused the chair to lose traction with the floor and it skittered away from her. She tumbled again, but this time Hugh was ready. He caught her against the wall with his good arm, barely stopping her from hitting the ground. He let her slide down until her feet touched the floor.

He didn't release her right away, and she stared up at him with wide, frightened eyes.

"You all right?" His voice was husky, and he tried to clear his throat, but there was nothing in there to clear. Her proximity and nothing else had changed his tone.

She nodded wordlessly.

A sudden urge to kiss her frown away reared in his chest. His hold on her tightened and he angled his body so it was more in front of her, pinning her to the wall. He wanted to hold her tight and never let her away from him.

She flattened her palm against his chest and gently pushed him away. Then she slipped to the side and out of his almost embrace. Her action was a silent and disappointing answer to his unspoken plea. She hopelessly smoothed skirts that had been wrinkled since she stepped out of the coach four days ago.

He looked up at the trap. Would all the commotion along the wall cause it to fall and knock him in the head? It might be a favor, for if he were addled, he would at least be able to keep himself away from Edna. Why couldn't he control himself around her the way he could with Catherine? They were no different from each other, both were women he was familiar with, both too good for him. Experience might even say Edna was a worse option for Hugh than was Catherine, for Edna had lived as a merchant in a big city where anything could be bought. Out here, where a family did most everything for themselves, Fay was still teaching Edna how to survive.

Edna dragged the chair back to its spot along the wall. It looked lonely without her in it. This whole cabin made him feel lonely. Lonely for Pete. Melancholy for the friend he'd lost. And Pete had lost so much. As bad off as Hugh's family was, many, like Pete, were worse off. Hugh's family had experienced tragedy, but no deaths. Like he'd said to Edna, love couldn't be monetized. Impractical as it was, he would choose love every time.

He went and checked the stove, throwing another log in, even though it was plenty full already. How long could he keep this up? Ignoring his feelings, enduring her close proximity, and not giving way to whatever snapped between them?

Edna said, "Tomorrow is Christmas." She watched out the window as though there was something to see out there other than boughs weighted with snow. "How are we going to get home?"

Hugh came and stood behind her. Memory from riding here made it so he could almost feel her lean against him, feel the set of her shoulders sitting perfectly between his. She might not be his, but he knew the feel of her better than any other woman.

It was a dangerous thought.

He stepped to the side to stop the image. "Pete will come back and we'll use his horse. Or Lachlan might've thought this was where I'd go." Hugh's stomach twisted. Lachlan was ill. Was he in his right mind? Was anyone informing him of Hugh's long absence? Was anyone consulting Hugh's brother, who alternately emptied his stomach into a bucket and slept all the day? Fay knew, too, but that girl was still as flighty as a sparrow, only brushing the tops of the grasses and never quite settling on the ground.

"You think they'll come for us?"

Hugh shrugged. "That, or Pete will come home and he can send word for us."

Edna turned to face Hugh, but the lines of her face were obscured in shadow. Almost all day long, the space needed a lantern. If Hugh owned this place, he would cut down the trees that towered so near, close enough that a bad storm might mean Pete was crushed in his sleep. But if he were here, Edna wouldn't be with him. Whose face would there be to see in the dark? Perhaps Pete wanted the trees. Perhaps they kept out the memories. Perhaps he didn't mind a harsh windstorm reuniting him with his family.

"But tomorrow is Christmas." Edna's voice was a broken whisper that split Hugh's chest like an ax in wood.

"I'm sorry you aren't in Chicago with your mama."

"It's not that. Pete won't be coming back tomorrow or the next day. He's likely visiting his family for the holiday. What if he isn't home until the New Year?"

Hugh almost laughed at her refusal to believe Pete wasn't with family. "We've got plenty of supplies."

"Hugh, we can't just stay here forever."

Her voice was high-pitched, desperate. Hugh wanted to wrap his arm around her. To press her against his wound and feel the pain of life. Something Jimmy no longer had.

"We won't. We're going home." Suddenly this cabin felt too dark, too isolated. Why hadn't he tried to get Pete back to Dragonfly Creek? It wasn't right for a human to live in a shadowy cave like this.

Edna pressed away from the window and walked around the cabin, pacing the small space. Finally she came back to him and gestured at his wound. "Let me put a clean bandage on."

Hugh cowered, as though guarding himself against her. "Just because you're restless doesn't mean you get to poke at me."

Edna marched closer and tugged at the collar of his shirt, stretching her neck to see down at his wound.

"Excuse me, miss. I feel most violated." He stayed his ground, wishing she'd use his fisted shirt to tug him flush against her.

Edna laughed. "We've not changed it yet today."

He narrowed his eyes. She was right, but in her agitated state, he doubted she'd be gentle. Perhaps her anxiety was the exact reason he should allow her to clean it. He could stand a little pain if it meant she settled down.

"All right, but the back first." He didn't like how she picked and poked at the stitches in the front. He started lifting the sling over his head, but Edna was there, and she lifted it the rest of the way over his head and slid it off. He watched her face, so serene after nearly throwing a tantrum in the cabin. It was possible she was like his mama, a woman who liked to stay busy, who got antsy if she didn't have her hands at work, or in Edna's case, in a batch of dough. Or—he chuckled—perhaps the idea of him in pain soothed her, the troublesome fox.

She helped him remove his shirt, and he stood with his back to her. He held the front bandage on as she removed the tie that held both bandages in place.

Her hands slipped off his skin and silence buzzed around him.

"What?" he asked, casting a look over his shoulder and trying to catch sight of her face. "Have I grown a tail?"

Her fingers briefly, gently, nudged his skin once more.

Shooting pain spread like ripples in a pond. He jerked away from her with a hiss.

She circled his body to stand before him, her face pinched and white as the snow that coated the earth. "It's gone sour." Her chin tightened and dimpled as she tried to still her quivering lip. "What if it gets worse? I don't have proper medicine here."

Hugh huffed, trying to joke so he didn't focus on the dark thoughts swirling. "I couldn't afford it anyway."

Edna let her head fall to one side and glowered at him.

"I'm not teasing you. We can't afford it on both accounts, so clean me up good, doc." He gestured for her to get behind him again.

She gave him a long, critical look before conceding. Without his shirt, his skin was cold, and goosebumps rose across his entire upper half. Her hands, like ice, didn't help. He tried not to move away from her touch, but it was uncomfortable in every way. Mostly in how he didn't want her to stop. She touched his bare shoulder, handling and moving him this way and that without propriety. It was a shame that, even though she could touch him like this, taking her hand would cause a shift in their world. The more he thought about it, the more he wanted her palm in his.

But too soon the image in his mind shifted from a loving wife to one with a worn dress. One who needed clothing and him with nothing to offer her. She and Fay would work something out, but it would be nothing like the fine fabrics she wore that had been bought in the city. Edna would smile and try to be grateful, but she would be disappointed. Possibly the disappointment wouldn't even have anything to do with him anymore, but with herself for settling when she could have found a better man.

Soon he smelled the tangy, medicinal scent of the salve she used. She clicked her tongue, her face appearing around his arm. "Let's move to the bed so this bandage will stay put while I tend the front."

They walked together, Edna following his movements with her fingers pressed against his wound. Pain pulsed through his shoulder, but it held him, like a fish hook snagged on a tree. If it weren't there, he feared what he might do to her. So far, this adventure had been just that. But if he pressed his mouth to hers, it would take off on an entirely different course, a stagecoach team running in whatever direction they pleased, with no knowledge of the cliff that could be over the next crest.

Hugh sat down and Edna climbed up onto the bed. As he laid down, she shifted to make room until she was kneeling in the center of the bed, with him lying along the edge.

Edna lifted the bandage from the front of his bullet wound. He heard a sticky sound and turned away.

"Oh, Hugh," she breathed.

He looked down, seeing splotches of red and yellow circling the tangle of black thread that was his stitches. He turned his gaze to her. The idea of that mess coming from his own body turned his stomach. "Did you say alcohol cleaned the wound?"

Her mouth worked, and her chin quivered as she took a moment to find words. "I don't know. I can't remember." Her voice held a desperation Hugh felt too keenly.

"We may need to try it."

Her eyes flew to his. "But it *hurt*."

He nodded. "This has festered, and it's too close to my chest to be easily cut off." He grinned.

She gave a weak smile. "How can you joke?"

"I've got a pretty girl leaning over me, thinkin' about spilling tears on my account."

She used the tips of her fingers to wipe at her eyes and sniffed.

He closed his eyes, letting his mouth spread in a grin. "I'd say it ain't all bad."

He risked a peek. She chewed her lip, staring at his shoulder in contemplation.

He closed them again, and rested his head on the pillow.

"How about you start by getting me a drink, then when I'm good and gone, you can pour it on me."

She gave a faint chuckle and climbed off the bed to pour him a shallow cup of Pete's alcohol. He sipped it, cringing with each swallow. Try as he might, he couldn't keep his eyes closed, not with her so near. He watched her every expression, every flutter of her hands as she gathered items from the cupboard.

She returned, and he watched as she poured alcohol on a clean cloth and dabbed at his wound. After she'd done so a few times, she stopped and lifted an eyebrow at him. "Are you calm because you're expecting it? Or because it hurts less?"

"Both, I suppose." His voice was tight as he held back a groan.

She set the cloth down and stared at the wound, chewing her bottom lip again.

"What?" he asked, trying to distract himself from watching her mouth.

"I can't decide. Do I leave the wound open to the air to help it dry? Or close it up to protect it from any dust or debris in the air?" She looked down at her hands and her fingertips were a chalky white. She brought the other hand level, running her thumb along the ghostly fingers. She brought them to her nose and sniffed. "Alcohol." She glanced up. "It left some of itself behind."

With a curt nod, she dabbed a generous amount of alcohol on the clean bandage. Then she gingerly laid it over Hugh's wound. "Maybe this will keep the outside cleaner. If the wound expels any liquid, it can wet the bandage and reactivate the alcohol?" Her words turned up at the end to form a sort of question.

Hugh shrugged. "Sound logic to me." He had no idea if the

alcohol would even do a thing to help the wound, but Edna did, and her tight, concerned look was melting away.

She glanced at the bandana she had used to hold both bandages against his skin. It looked filthy compared to everything else. "You need a bath."

Hugh laughed. "I won't argue. Would you like me to run down to the creek?"

Edna's eyes flew open. He laughed harder until he groaned, reaching for his bad shoulder.

"Does it hurt? Oh, Hugh, what are we going to do?"

The way she said his name was like a breath. He wanted to hear her say it again and again. *Oh, Hugh.* He looked up at her. "Pete will be here soon." To save Hugh from both an infection and from a broken heart. While they'd been in this cabin, he'd been giving away his heart in small doses. Soon, she would hold all of him in her tiny palm.

Her eyes were big, scared. "You don't know that. He could be gone another two weeks."

She did paint a grim picture. As much as he'd like to spend another two weeks under Edna's gentle hand, their families would be worried sick, and with Lachlan ill, he was needed on their farm. He tried to picture what they were doing without him. No doubt Fay and Mama were doing Lachlan's chores. The Grahams would be fending for themselves without his or Fay's help.

He stopped the images, refusing to allow them to carry him away. "Pete hates being in town. He's not going to be gone for long."

"I still think he must be visiting *someone* for Christmas." Her voice hitched higher with panic.

Hugh leveled her with a look. "Trust me. Pete never stays for long. He can't stand people."

Edna cocked her head, shifting off her knees and onto her hip. "He manages to put up with you."

He liked her sitting over him like this, teasing him. His bandage was still lightly settled on his shoulder. If he sat up, it would fall to the ground.

"You going to bandage me up, or will I have to lie here all day?"

Edna lifted the bandana in her hands. "It's filthy."

Hugh pointed his chin at the drawer under the bedside table. "He might have a clean one in there."

Edna rooted around the drawer and other shelves before coming up with a dingy blue cloth. "It's the best he has."

Hugh nodded and tried to ignore the way the bed jostled under her weight. Not because it pained him, but because it made him imagine another life where she might be climbing into bed as something other than his nursemaid.

She tied the bandage and helped him into his shirt. Hurt arm first, then his good arm, then she slipped it over his head. She climbed off the bed and waved him over. "Sit on the edge. I'll do your buttons."

He placed his boots on the floor and raised his chin so she could button him up. The buttons were small and impossible to do without using his left hand. When she finished, she placed a flat palm against his chest. "Tell me if your bandage feels … wrong."

Hugh smiled. "Yes, captain."

She turned and leaned against the bed, they're arms nearly touching. If he dared, he could wrap his arm around her and kiss the top of her head. He shook the idea away. Where was it all coming from? This playing house was addling his brains.

Edna glanced up at him, "Tomorrow is Christmas. We should do something to celebrate."

Hugh chuckled. "I'm fresh out of gifts."

Edna nodded, picking at her nails. "You're right. It was a silly idea."

The way her face fell had him leaning closer, her shoulder brushed against his arm. "It wasn't silly. I'll come up with something."

"You can't." She waved her hand at his injured arm.

Hugh straightened. "Is that a challenge?"

She laughed. "No. I don't know what I can give either. I'm already making you food and taking care of you. What more can I offer?"

Hugh could think of one thing he'd love for her to offer. He glued his gaze to hers so he wouldn't sneak a look at her lips and give himself away. "You'll think of something."

She glanced around the cabin. "I'm going to go collect a few pine boughs to decorate." Standing, she moved toward the door and slid into her coat.

Hugh called after her, "Better make sure there aren't any pests in those boughs. Pete won't thank you for inviting a family of mantises into his place."

She smirked at him and closed the door behind herself. The image of her stayed long after she'd gone. He ran a hand through his hair and sighed. Tilting his head back, he stared at the ceiling, at the wood grain so tight together, then separating around a knot. With closed eyes he prayed, *Please Lord, let Pete return soon.*

16

EDNA WOKE in the morning curled around Hugh's backside. His body expanded like a rising loaf of bread, then contracted again with each breath .With her face pressed against his back, she felt every pump of his heart, how every inhale and exhale moved his body. It took all her willpower to move away from his heat. She scrunched her face at the idea of him waking up and learning she'd snuggled against him in the night. But moving wasn't easy. He was so heavy the mattress dipped where he lay, and rolling away was impossible. She'd have to push away from his back to get anywhere, and that would surely wake him.

She lay there, breathing against the planes of his shoulder blades. If he'd been drunk and she could guarantee he wouldn't wake, she might have just wrapped her arms around him and enjoyed his warmth. What would it be like to wake to a man every morning? A man whom she didn't have to fear rousing. Possibly she'd even wake in *his* arms, secure in his love for her.

She sighed. Now was no time to wish for a husband. If she'd ever thought herself ready to entertain suitors, these last few days had taught her otherwise. She was still too weak where men were concerned. But she was beginning to wonder whether she would ever be strong. Perhaps girls with dead papas grow up to be desperate women, and there was nothing to be done about it. No amount of self-control could replace what mortality had claimed.

The white strip of the bandage glowed along Hugh's neckline, showing under the collar of his shirt. Perhaps her wound had festered too. Perhaps taking Brandon away so suddenly had been taking the bandage off too soon, and now she was dealing with a festering bit of flesh that begged to be cleaned. She huffed in amusement. Should she start Christmas off with a nice glass of Pete's homemade alcohol to clean the festering in her heart?

She could imagine Hugh's expression if she did so. She'd been older when she learned proper women didn't drink and never in company. Her mama had often finished the day with a bit of the amber liquid. She would drink it slowly, her swollen feet propped on the hearth. Edna could remember the ache in her own feet from a day's work in the bakery. She could remember going to bed when there were still children playing in the street, only to wake before the birds.

It hadn't been an easy life, but her mama taught her that hard work was the American Dream.

Light as a feather, Edna ran her middle finger along Hugh's back. It was hard with muscle, and she imagined in the summer it would be tanned by the sun. She wanted to feel the calluses on his hands, to match them with her own. She pulled her hand back, tucking it into her chest. This man wasn't hers to touch. He wasn't even Catherine's. He belonged to his family and nobody else.

And who did Edna belong to? Not *her* family. She couldn't even return home without dread weighing her in her middle like a stone in a pond. Did that mean she still belonged to Brandon? He was still controlling her choices, even this far away.

Edna frowned at having missed her train to Chicago. The only real benefit from being forced to visit was that she'd have been able to talk with Frederick, to pick his brain about an affordable cure for Lachlan. Something she could learn the recipe for and make herself, rather than the Morrises paying the expensive fees to the apothecary in Billings.

She would have to write to Frederick again when she returned to Aster Ridge, beg him to forgive her for being such a terrible friend, for allowing Brandon to make her choose between them, and for choosing wrong. She drew a ragged breath. Was it wrong when she knew if she had gone back in time she would have chosen the same path? Why had she been so lonely? She wasn't lonely out here in Montana, and she wasn't just thinking about the man whose legs were pressed against her own. She had friends. But, mostly, she *liked* herself out here. She couldn't remember when that had stopped in Chicago. But here, with Hugh, she felt funny again. Lighter. Being with Brandon had been the start of her believing women had a place and they couldn't do every-thing. Here, she felt capable once more. She felt like there was a future waiting for her, and it burned bright, filled with a man who teased her and whom she teased right back.

She ran her gaze up Hugh's back and to his hair. It had a slight wave to it. If it were long, it would be the envy of all the girls. She wanted to run her fingers along his scalp. She wanted to run her hands over all of him. She gulped, shoving that thought deep into darkness, and risked waking him by roughly rolling away and climbing out of the covers. The cold floor shocked her enough to clear away her daydreams.

She threw a log in the stove and padded over to the hook for her shawl. She'd just wrapped it around her shoulders when Hugh sucked in a yawn and said, "Good morning."

Edna wanted to crawl back into the bed. To hold him and pretend just for today that he was hers. Could she ask for *him* for Christmas?

Hugh sat up, setting his feet on the floor. He slept on the open side and had no need to climb over anyone to get out of bed. He lowered one thick eyebrow. "What are you smiling about?"

Edna tucked her lips between her teeth, but they seemed intent on laughter. "Merry Christmas."

Hugh grinned, then ran a hand over his face, itching at the whiskers and drawing her gaze to his chin and mouth. While they were stranded in this cabin, he was all hers and she his. They belonged to one another, at least for now.

He sucked in a long breath and stretched his back. "Merry Christmas. Shall we exchange gifts? Or wait until after breakfast?" Hugh's eyes darted aimlessly around the room.

Edna couldn't wait to find out about whatever was making him nervous. "Let's exchange them now." She practically bounced on her toes.

His throat bobbed, and she must be the cruelest of women, because his anxiety gave her a thrill.

Hugh stood and tucked his shirt into his pants while Edna went to the shelf where she'd found the furry slippers. She plucked them up and held them behind her back.

"Are you ready for your gift?" she asked.

Hugh stretched his neck as though he could see behind her. "Ye-es." He drew the word out like he wasn't quite sure.

Edna sat on the bed, realizing she was inappropriately dressed in her shift and shawl, but formalities had disappeared, for it was Christmas. Hugh sat too, giving her an expectant look.

She pulled the slippers from behind her and held them out to Hugh.

They were made from a kind of grayish brown fur and

were turned so the furry side was in and the tanned leather was out. They reminded her of a winter version of the leathery shoes the natives wore.

Hugh took them from her and laughed. "You cannot give these to me. They aren't even yours."

Edna grimaced. "Well, I'm afraid my gift does require a bit of work on your part."

Hugh laughed. "Like buying them from Pete?"

Edna laughed too. "No, I want to *make* these for you, but I'll need to buy a pelt from you first."

Hugh looked closer, running his thumb along the stitching above the toes. Edna had done the same when she found them. Had even tried to envision a paper pattern of the way the pelt had been cut.

She glanced back at Hugh, chewing her lip while she waited to see if he thought her gift ridiculous. After all, slippers like this would go for a fortune in the city. But, out here, it seemed pelts were everywhere. Along the collar of every woman's coat, even hanging on interior walls for decoration. "Would you like a pair?"

Hugh's gaze snapped to her, and his cheeks colored. "Yes. I think I would."

He grinned wide, easing the nervousness she held in her chest. She cupped her hands and raised her brows expectantly.

"Oh, did you mean for me to give you a gift as well?"

She nodded vigorously. She had never been too keen on gifts. But the challenge of coming up with something from this stranger's cabin had changed that. She couldn't wait to see what Hugh had come up with.

His words were slow when he spoke, and as she listened, her heart nearly beat out of her chest. "I thought to carve you a little something, but there wasn't enough time for anything intricate." He stood and poured himself a cup of water. He cleared his throat, then drank, and cleared it again.

Edna waved away his apologies, anxious for whatever was to come. But then her shoulders dipped. Was he telling her he'd not been able to come up with anything on such short notice? She swallowed, lowering her hands. It had been awfully rude of her to expect something, like a baby bird when its mother returns to the nest. She was about to apologize when Hugh spoke again.

"I couldn't do much with you always about and … my arm." He jiggled his bad arm as he sat back on the bed.

Edna nodded. Her gift had been rather sorry, too. It wasn't even his. It was merely going back up on the shelf where she'd found it.

"I need you to turn around."

Edna's gaze snapped to him.

He spun his finger around, in instruction for her to turn away. Slowly, she turned on the mattress so her back was facing him. She cast a look over her shoulder, but he nudged her back again. "No peeking."

"Okay." She settled in for… what? Was he going to plait her hair?

He cleared his throat one last time. And sang.

His voice was a lovely baritone. Edna twisted to look at him but he pushed at her shoulder, and she turned back once more. She couldn't even resent him for not letting her look at him because her heart was soaring to the tune, dancing on each note, each word of the story. The song told of two lost lovers finding their way to one another.

She recognized the tune as the one he had been humming, the song he would never sing when asked. His refusal had fooled her into believing he was shy about his voice. She would never have believed he was hiding this buttery pool. She wanted to dive in and swim around in it.

The words were as beautiful as his voice, and they caused goosebumps to raise on her arms. She tugged her shawl tighter.

He finished, and the silence in the cabin felt like a hand on her heart, not gripping, but a gentle press. A tear cascaded down Edna's cheek, and she wiped it away. Hugh shifted behind her, and she turned and faced him. "That was beautiful." She sniffed, wanting him to sing it again. "Can I sit next to you on Sunday?"

He laughed. "We might be holding a worship of our own right here."

"That's just fine with me." She glanced around the space. "I wouldn't mind staying here for the rest of my days."

A look she couldn't identify crossed his face. She'd said too much. Now he thought she was in love with him, which perhaps she was, but he had made it very clear that no woman was for him.

EDNA STOOD and found her clothes. Hugh turned his back as she dressed. He replayed her words in his mind: *I wouldn't mind staying here for the rest of my days.* Could she truly be content here, with only basic needs met? Fay surely wouldn't, and he doubted Eloise would have done it either. He didn't know a single woman who would truly trade a life of convenience for one of hard work.

He spoke loud enough that she could hear while she dressed. "Is the work harder at Aster Ridge than it was in Chicago?"

Edna chuckled. "No. Mama had me up before dawn baking, then I ran the register all day."

He could easily imagine her behind a shiny counter with a glittering cash register in front of her. The breads might have been fine, but he didn't doubt there was more than one customer who came to flirt with the pretty girl at the front of the shop. An unfamiliar wave washed over him. Jealousy?

"Sounds like a lot of work. Is that why you left? Why you don't want to go back?"

He felt, rather than saw, her freeze. Maybe he noticed it because he expected her to react to any mention of home.

"My mama is wonderful, and there are few things I'd like more than to see her."

"But…"

Edna walked around and glared at him. "Do you think I'm afraid of hard work? I understand out here"—she gestured widely, and he understood she meant in Montana—"there are few things worse than a person who avoids work." She met his gaze and narrowed her eyes. "Are you saying I'm lazy?"

Hugh shook his head. He went to answer, but she cut him off.

"Home isn't just Mama. It's Chicago. It's the house and the people. There's more to it. Now stop pestering me and get me some water from the creek."

She passed him a bucket, and he obeyed the captain, even saluting her and earning himself a frosty glare.

He chuckled as he walked to the creek, remembering her fiery reaction to the idea that he considered her lazy. There were many things he'd grown to admire about Edna, her humor, her kindness, her determination. But hard work was the one trait that had been important to him, even before he met her. It was the one thing that if she didn't have it, he might not have been able to picture a life with her even in his wildest imaginations. As it was, his imagination was running away with him more and more, and he wasn't inclined to rein it in.

17

Just as he had the first time, Hugh regretted pressing Edna about Chicago. That was the last time. He would leave it alone and let her keep her secrets to herself. He filled the bucket and, as he walked back, an idea occurred to him. There was another gift he could have given and he now wished he'd thought of it sooner. It would have been much less embarrassing.

He entered the cabin and set the bucket on the table. "I have another gift for you."

She set two plates on the table, each loaded with a bit of hash. She gestured for him to sit.

He set the bucket on the ground and sat down. "I'd like to fill Pete's tub and let you have a bath."

Edna stilled, bright spots blooming on each cheek. She stared at him, her face unreadable.

"If that's inappropriate, I'm sorry. I just...it's not easy hauling all that water. I would have done it sooner, but..." He pointed lamely to his shoulder.

Edna seemed to shake herself. "I'd love one." She nodded

at him. "You could use one yourself. Especially after you haul all the water."

Hugh laughed, glad she could still tease him. He hadn't realized how inappropriate his offer would sound.

They said grace, and before he dug into his food, Hugh filled the kettle and set it on the stove to start warming.

"I suppose you're going to stand out in the freezing cold while I bathe in here?" Edna looked at him with raised brows.

"Well, don't take your time."

Edna laughed. "We could hang a blanket and create a private space."

Hugh shook his head. "There's plenty for me to do outside." He didn't know what those things were, but he wouldn't test the limits of her ruined reputation. Nor would he tempt his self-control. He'd dreamed of her last night. His imagination hadn't even been creative. She was in the kitchen back home, and she turned around with such love on her face. It was apparent she was there as his wife and welcoming him home for the day. The irony was that he'd been forced awake from the dream by the very woman he'd wanted to stay asleep for.

When it was time, Hugh borrowed an old knit cap of Pete's and set his own hat over top. He started on Pete's tiny barn. With a hammer, he knocked in loose nails and tightened hinges. There really wasn't much to do. No doubt, out here Pete had plenty of time and little to occupy him. Hugh wondered if Pete had left any traps set while he was away. If he did, it might indicate he intended to be home sooner rather than later.

Hugh wasn't lying when he said he didn't think Pete was staying anywhere for Christmas. Might be that Pete didn't even know it *was* Christmas, only that it was December.

He walked along the path where he knew Pete set traps.

He couldn't help but remember walking this path with both Pete and Jimmy. The two friends started spending more time out here after Jimmy's mama died and his sisters moved away.

Jimmy was one of those babies who had come when his parents thought they were done with children. He grew up with siblings, but they were all much older than him, and most days he said it felt like he was an only child. His mama doted on him, which only made it harder when they had to put her in the ground. Hugh's chest clenched. He sent up a prayer of gratitude that his family all still lived. A miracle, that. Not even a babe lost. It was rare in these parts.

When he came across no traps, he turned back. Surely Edna had finished and, hopefully, the water would still be a bit warm.

He stepped over the last small hill and a dog yapped. Hugh's feet moved, taking him to the house at a clip, before his mind had even made sense of the situation. A horse was tethered to the post and a man stood on the porch. "Hey!" Hugh shouted. Shock pulsed rigid fear through every muscle, but then he got a good look at the dog as it bounded toward him. He would know it anywhere—it was Jimmy's dog, Bee.

The man turned and Hugh spotted Pete's scraggly form with a pistol pointed at Hugh's heart. Bee had stopped barking and was wagging her tail wildly, trying to jump up on Hugh.

Hugh raised both hands in the air to show he held no weapons. "Pete, it's me. Hugh Morris."

Pete uncocked the gun and slid it into its holster. He jutted a thumb over his shoulder. "That your girl in there?"

A thousand scenarios were running through Hugh's mind about what had transpired while he was on the trapline. He tripped over his words as he climbed the steps to the porch.

He pulled Pete into his arms, holding the man fiercely, his throat thick with emotion. "You live too far out here."

They broke apart. "Not far enough, I say. There's a bit of vermin creeping around."

Hugh chuckled. "Surely I'm not *that* unwelcome." Hugh strode to the door. He knocked twice and called, "Edna, Pete and I are out here waiting."

The door opened and a fully-dressed Edna scowled through it. "Where *were* you?" she hissed.

"I was out checking traps. I guess I went a bit too far."

Edna's eyes flashed to Pete and then back to Hugh. "This is Pete?"

Hugh nodded.

She threw her shoulders back. "Sorry I hollered at you. I didn't expect…you."

Hugh didn't know if she meant the grizzled old man, or anyone at all. He desperately wanted to ask what had happened. Had Pete seen…everything?

Edna stepped to the side, opening the door wider as she did so, like a gracious host letting in two strays.

The tub was tucked into the shadows by the bed, and Hugh hoped the darkness had acted in Edna's favor.

"I was taking Ms. Archer to Billings when we were set upon by three riders."

Pete slid his gaze away from Edna and narrowed his eyes at Hugh. "You couldn't take three men?"

Hugh chuckled. "It was pouring rain, and I wasn't expecting any trouble. I figured most would be inside by a fire."

"The desperate never rest."

"And I was driving a team of four. When I tried to shoot, the horses veered and I might have killed her by letting the coach tip."

Pete sniffed. "I've plenty of supplies that need unloading."

"Of course." Hugh followed Pete outside.

They made their way to the wagon. When they were safely out of Edna's hearing, Hugh leaned closer to Pete. "You didn't...see anything?"

"Your girl screamed right good. I knew from the chimney smoke I'd find someone inside. I didn't expect it to be a lady. I backed right out and waited." Pete chuckled. "Don't know what I was waiting *for*. If you hadn't turned up, I might have waited until spring."

Hugh laughed. "You always were patient."

"Where's your mount?"

"Dead." Hugh jerked his head toward the south. "Hit by a bullet. We rode it hard as far as we could."

Pete nodded toward Hugh's arm. "Looks like you might've been hit yourself."

Hugh hefted a sack with his good arm. "I can still work."

They took several trips unloading the wagon, then put Pete's horse safely in the barn. Once the wagon was empty, they made their way inside. Walking right to the stove, they stood on either side, their hands outstretched to remove the chill from their fingers.

Pete called to Edna over his shoulder. "There's a turkey. I thought to dry it, but with two guests, I suppose we can cook it and have ourselves a feast."

Edna winced. "I'm afraid we've helped ourselves to your food. You should save the bird for yourself."

Pete waved her away. "I'm just one man. I don't eat much."

The way his shirt hung on his shoulders told Hugh he wasn't eating enough.

Pete nodded toward Hugh's arm. "Let's have a look, son."

Hugh obliged, wincing at the pain of lifting his arm too high, and wishing Edna was helping him remove his shirt. She'd been coddling him these last few days, and he hadn't even realized.

Pete removed the bandage, which they hadn't changed this morning. Hugh had hoped to change it after his bath. He glanced at the tub, the water cold now. One or two pots of hot water might do the trick. No doubt Pete had the same idea.

"You need a shave." Hugh chucked Pete's chin, and the man smiled, his teeth bright through the tangle of hair.

Pete ran a hand along the length of his beard. "I wasn't expecting company. Otherwise I might have done so."

"No, you wouldn't have." Hugh laughed, then winced as Pete poked at his wound. "Infection is setting in."

Edna came over, hands on her hips. "I found the calendula you had in the cupboard, and alcohol seems to be helping, but I didn't know what else to use."

Pete cast a look over his shoulder. "Crush a few cloves of garlic and bring them over." Pete looked at Hugh. "You should get back to town."

"Been wishing for it, but with the snow and no horse... I'm glad you're back."

"Take Como, but bring her right back."

Hugh knew what a sacrifice it was for Pete to lend his horse. He knew all too well how stranded a body was out here without one. If anything happened to Pete, he would die alone without the chance to get himself help.

"I will. Can he take two?"

Pete nodded. "Just go easy. He's not as young as he used to be."

Hugh eyed the gray in Pete's hair as he tended Hugh's shoulder. "He's not the only one. I think your hair will be white by next year."

Pete gestured for Hugh to turn around so he could see the other side. "Last winter wasn't easy."

"I don't expect many of them are. Ever thought about coming back? You can stay out of town. Fay would bring you treats and Papa would love a bit of company now and then."

"How is your pa?"

"A bit of a sickness in his chest, but no worse than what comes every winter."

"Winter ain't easy in town either."

"No, I suppose it isn't. But there's help if it's needed."

Edna returned with the garlic. Pete turned Hugh around again before taking a slick of the calendula balm and smearing it with garlic before wiping it on Hugh's shoulder. He placed the old bandage over top and Hugh watched as Edna opened her mouth to protest and stopped herself. They met eyes over Pete's shoulder and smiled at one another. He supposed if the infection was too deep, he'd be paying for a doctor's visit anyway.

"Did you hear? Pete's letting us take his horse."

Edna's face transformed as she gave Pete a heartfelt smile. "Oh, Pete. Thank you."

"Don't see as I've much of a choice. I can't keep you two here eating all my stores."

Edna's face fell.

Hugh laughed. "I hope you don't expect me to go easy on the turkey. We're missing Christmas with our families."

Pete started. "It's Christmas?"

Hugh smiled. "I wondered if you knew." His smug gaze slid to Edna.

"Course I knew. Why'd you think I suggested eating the bird?"

"I think you suggested it because you had a woman here to cook it for you. You're in luck—she's the best baker I know."

Pete harrumphed and finished applying the garlic to the back of his wound. Then he tied the bandana on, tight enough that Hugh winced.

Pete lifted the bucket from the ground. "I'm going for a bit of water. I want to use what's left of that tub."

When he was gone Edna went to Hugh. "Let me loosen that bandana."

"It's fine."

Edna let her head fall to the side. "I saw your face when he tied it." She waved him over and tugged the collar of his shirt over to adjust the tie. He watched her as she worked, her face upturned and distracted. Why hadn't he looked at her more? They were heading home tomorrow, and he couldn't imagine a world where they would ever be this close again.

Hugh slid his hands from her elbows, up her arms. "Thank you. For taking care of me."

Edna scoffed and dropped her hands, apparently finished with the tie. She took a small step back, but Hugh kept hold of her shoulders.

She looked him in the eyes. "You took care of me too. Remember?" She held her hands up like two pistols, her first finger aiming right at Hugh's chest.

"I shouldn't have taken you without Lachlan."

Edna's brows creased. "It's not your fault. I waited until the last moment. And you can't take responsibility for what those men did."

"No, but I knew better. I thought about the danger of driving alone, and I didn't speak up."

Edna pinched the front of his shirt and started redoing the buttons. "I forgive you." But it felt more like she was absolving him. "We'll be home tomorrow and everyone will know we are safe."

She was right. Everyone deserved to know they were safe. So why did the prospect of going home weigh heavy on his heart?

18

THEY PULLED the table to the bed and Edna and Hugh sat on the mattress while Pete sat in his one chair. They had finished dinner, and Hugh had fulfilled his promise to eat his fill. Edna couldn't believe how much food the man could eat. Apparently, she'd been starving him this whole time with measly portions.

They all sat in the contented silence that comes after a feast, smiles on their lips and hands on their stomachs. Pete's dog, Bee, raised her head at the door. Both men froze, and Pete slowly rose from his seat. He moved on silent feet to where his rifle leaned against the wall. His gaze flicked to his boots, but he didn't put them on.

Hugh stood, too, and his throat bobbed. Edna grabbed a fistful of his sleeve. "Hugh." She whispered, her voice cracking.

"Get under the bed."

His voice held no inflection, just a calm that nearly crackled with command. She was on her knees at the side of the bed when Pete threw open the door and pointed his rifle into the inky dark. "Who's there?" he shouted into the night.

Bee stood at his heels, growling. Edna shifted backward until only her nose could be seen.

A voice shouted back, distant, as though they'd been checking the cabin from afar. "We're lookin' for a man. Shot two of us."

"Nobody like that here. Best you get on your way or more'n two of you will be shot."

"Smells mighty nice round here. Don't suppose you have any to spare for a lonely traveler?"

"Go on!" Pete yelled back, and his voice was so gruff, Edna ducked closer to the bed. If she had to, it would only take a second to duck her head underneath. But the prospect of not seeing what was happening was too frightening.

The voice rose again from the dark. "It's Christmas. Are you going to turn away a few men looking for an inn?"

"Unless one of you is carrying a babe in your belly, you best be off 'fore I send one of you to meet your Maker."

The night hung still. No men spoke. Hugh stood near Edna, his boots blocking her view of anything besides the pistol he held at the ready.

"Go on!" With a whistle and wave, Pete sent Bee out into the night and closed the door, laying a board across to bar it shut. Bars on the outside, bars on the inside. This was a veritable fortress.

Hugh reached a hand out to Edna and helped her to rise. Edna stared at the closed door, knowing Pete's loyal dog was out there with the very men who had sent Hugh and her here. "Won't they hurt her?"

Pete clicked his tongue. "Might, but better her than us." He hung towels over the windows, blocking out the ability for those men to see inside.

The statement was so callused it stole Edna's words. The winters weren't the only harsh thing out here. She watched in silence as he covered the windows, grateful, for the first time, that there were few and they were small.

"She'll come back when they've gone far enough." He glanced at Hugh's pistol. "That ain't going to do much in a shootout."

Hugh set it on the table. "This and one more is all I've got. The rifle stayed with the coach. As far as I know, it's out there now, about to be used against us."

Pete sat down again, leaning his rifle against the table. "Suppose it's better than nothing. Was it the men who took your coach?"

Hugh leaned against the bed, crossing his ankles. "Suppose so. I can't rightly say without seeing them. Might not be able to tell even if I was standing face-to-face with one of 'em."

Pete laid his hand on the table, within reach of the rifle if he needed it in a snap. "They're lookin' for you. Did you kill any of their men?"

"Hit two, maybe I killed one."

Edna slid her hand along the mattress and overlapped Hugh's pinkie with her own. He lifted his hand and interlaced their fingers, holding hers tight as though he appreciated the comfort. Or perhaps he was just afraid for her. Out here, men risked death. Women risked much worse.

She looked around the cabin. She'd need a better hiding place than under the bed. Any heathen would check there first.

Pete stood. "Let's douse the lights. I feel like I'm on display." He glanced at the covered windows, but there were still cracks around the edges. If the travelers got real close, they could look inside. He walked over to his pack, which leaned against the wall by the door, discarded in the fuss of frightening Edna, and pulled out a thick buffalo skin. With a snap he rolled it out and set up a bed using the rest of his traveling gear. Edna imagined this was much like what he did when he was on the road. "You two take the bed. I'll be fine down here."

Hugh stood, releasing Edna's hand as he stammered. He never got out a real word before Pete cut him off. "I know you've been sharing the bed. It ain't warm enough in here this time of year. Samantha was always at me to get a bigger stove."

"She was a wise woman." Hugh said, and the soft tone of his voice made Edna wish for his hand in hers once more.

"I know such a situation ain't right in town, but things are different out here." He leveled a look at Edna. "If we get in a tight spot, you climb out that window." He stared pointedly at the window closest to the bed. "That's your best chance." He looked at Hugh. "Can she shoot?"

Hugh shook his head. "I should'a taught her."

"No time now." He nodded at Hugh, "You sleep on the outside. I don't want those men using her against us."

Edna's throat went dry. "D'you think they're coming in here?"

"Only one man fits through that doorway at a time, and I'll be waiting on the other side."

He dragged his chair so it was several feet in front of the door. He sat down and laid his rifle across his lap. He turned his head slightly and said, "Get to bed. I'll be waking you when it's your turn."

Edna and Hugh moved the table away from the bed and Edna had half a mind to lay it down to bar the door. She was glad to not be sleeping alone. Propriety meant nothing right now. She wanted to be guarded and protected. Hugh lay on top of the blankets, and his head rested against the headboard.

Edna climbed under the quilts and whispered, "You heard Pete. You need to sleep."

"Can't sleep, not with those men out there."

"You can close your eyes and rest."

He closed his eyes but Edna tugged at the blankets, tight under his weight. "Hugh."

He opened his eyes again and drew in a breath through his nose. When he exhaled, he climbed off the bed and back in, this time under the covers. Edna scooted until she lay on her side, her whole front pressed against the side of his body.

"I'm scared, too." She breathed in, the scent of the garlic paste covering his bullet wound, burning her nose. The smell also brought comfort, for Pete had brought solutions with him. She shuddered to think where they would be without Bee's listening ear, without Pete's long-barreled rifle.

He reached his good arm across his body until just the tips of his fingers rested on her waist. "Pete's right. No man is going to try barging in here, not when he doesn't know what he'll find."

The last bit of flame in the downturned lantern dimmed and winked out, leaving them in total blackness. Edna found Hugh's hand and weaved her fingers through his. She closed her eyes, but her heart pounded in her chest. None of them would sleep well tonight.

MORNING CAME, and Hugh's stiff body ached from little sleep and much longing for Edna. When he was on watch, his body leaned toward the bed, as though wishing to be near her once more.

Bee had returned in the night with a yip. Pete rose and let her in, and she laid at the legs of the watch chair, no matter which man occupied it. She'd been calm, and with her as guard, Hugh's shoulders eased. The men must truly have gone off.

Pete rose at the first crack of sunlight and removed the bars from the door. He and Hugh went out to saddle the horse. When Pete buckled on his rifle scabbard, Hugh reached out and laid a hand on Pete's arm. "You need that gun."

Pete continued buckling the straps. "You need it more. I've got walls. Besides, I ain't gonna be the one who sends you out to the wolves without protection. Your mama doesn't need any more grief."

"She's bound to send me with a wagon's worth of appreciation."

"Don't let her waste anything on me. Your family would have done the same for my Jimmy." Pete reached into his inner pocket and drew out a fabric pouch. Pressing it into Hugh's hands, he said, "That's a bit of medicine. Hopefully you won't need the doc to visit." He nodded toward Hugh's shoulder.

Hugh slapped Pete on the back and thanked him as they made their way back inside the cabin. Edna was awake and heating up a bit of mash with turkey for breakfast.

Pete spooned himself a bite and spoke through a full mouth. "*You're* welcome to stay if you keep cooking like this."

"This isn't my best. I'm a baker, sir, and I'll send a few things back with Hugh when he returns your horse."

Before long, it was time to leave. Edna knelt on the floor by Bee, who barely lifted her head in appreciation. "I'm glad you're okay, girl." Edna scratched the dog behind her ears.

Then she stood and smiled at Pete, who pulled a square of blue fabric from his pocket, a match to the bandana that held Hugh's bandages in place. He snapped it open, then wrapped it twice around Edna's neck and tied it off. "That'll keep the chill off your neck."

Edna touched the fabric, a shimmer to her eyes, then tucked herself into Pete's arms for a hug.

Hugh watched her with awe, admiring her ability to converse with rich folks like the Grahams, and yet charm rough old Pete. It was a true talent. He imagined she'd used the skill often in her mother's bakery. But he didn't like to picture her there. He wanted to continue picturing her in his home, but he would settle for Della's kitchen or helping her haul goats home. So long as she stayed safe and close, that was enough.

19

HUGH RODE BEHIND HER. Far too close. Closer than he'd been when they made their way to Pete's with a wounded Hugh and on a dying horse. When Edna had been on the verge of closing her eyes and refusing to open them again.

Had there really been more room before? A saddle was only so big. Perhaps it was their time together changing this familiar scene. Everything with Hugh had changed. She knew too much about him now. Had slept next to him. Had clung to him. Only to go back and...what? Pretend none of it ever happened? If they spoke of it, her reputation would be ruined. If they ignored it, would it become some distant memory, a dream from a lifetime ago? That thought tugged the corners of her mouth into a frown.

What did she want? For Hugh to plant his boots on the boardwalk in front of town hall and confess all that had transpired? The bath which had nearly been interrupted by Pete entering the cabin, the shirtless doctoring, the cozy nights. The thought brought the smallest of smiles. Perhaps because it was absurd, but maybe because if Hugh ruined her, he would marry her. She did not doubt that.

Hugh had told her she could catch a number of men in town, but even the ones who fancied her wouldn't throw their hat in with her once they learned how she'd spent her last few days. At least not until they were certain she wasn't carrying Hugh's child in her belly.

Her face heated at the thought of Hugh's baby growing inside her. She was certain he wouldn't refuse to marry her then. He might even be happy with her. She knew enough to know when a man found her attractive. And they'd spent these last days in one another's company. For Edna it had been quite pleasant. Almost like when she played house as a little girl. Only it was Pete's stores they'd been eating, and Hugh had been nursing a bullet wound. None of the things she'd experienced had been how she'd played house as a child. They also hadn't been like real life, at least not the life she'd lived.

But something in her chest told her that, real or pretend, what they'd experienced didn't negate the truth that they would be more than content as companions. Her heart. *That* was the thing in her chest telling this to her. Her traitorous heart. It had never been one to obey. She mentally wrapped it in a too-tight bandage and told it to be still. But even as she did so, she noted that the blue of the bandage she'd imagined, matched Hugh's.

If she wanted to keep her promise to never fall for a man who elicited strong emotions, she had best stay farther from Hugh than before. She needed to move out of Aster Ridge. Maybe out of Montana.

Hugh stopped at a stream to water the horse. Edna climbed off after him, pacing to stretch her legs. The snow was older now, and the top had formed a thin layer of ice. Every step hovered for a moment before crunching down. Her boots were already unsalvageable, so there was no use in taking care where she stepped. When she got back to Dragonfly Creek, she would order herself a new pair. She looked up at the snow-covered trees. As they'd ridden, she'd seen the snow crash down, sprinkling the other branches with the snow it could no longer carry. Was that what a family was? One unit, where each part held their weight for as long as they could. Then when it became too much, it released its burden, only for the rest to take the weight.

Hugh's voice came from behind her. "Beautiful, isn't it?"

Edna turned. He stood closer than she'd expected, and she took a step back. She followed his gaze back up the trees. He must have seen this view a thousand times. "Do you often trap in the winter?"

"As much as I can. The winter fur are the warmest pelts, and they catch the best price."

"You've not gone yet this winter."

"No. Too much to do. And the Grahams have plenty of work. Perhaps trapping is a boy's dream."

"Pete makes a living from it."

Hugh huffed in amusement. "Yes, well, Pete feeds only himself, and I can't say he's better off for it."

Edna laughed. She found Pete both unnerving and somehow charming because of his oddness. A sprinkle of snow fell from the branch above Edna, and she closed her eyes against it, only to find the sensation of falling snow on her face much more enjoyable than the sodden trek in the rain.

Hugh took a crunching step nearer and dusted the snow from her collar and hair. She opened her eyes, meeting his dark irises flecked with gold. Rather than step away again, he let his hand hover near her ear. He stared into her, waiting. Edna licked her lips and swallowed. What was he waiting for? What did he want? Not her. He'd made that entirely too clear.

And yet, she stared at his mouth, his lips parted in the

middle. She imagined what it would be to feel them against her own. Warm and soft. That was Hugh, he was comfort and care. Injured as he was, she was safe from the world as long as he was near. Her heart was the problem. That wasn't safe, it was very much in danger of being broken. It needed distance or it would tumble down to a place she couldn't reach.

Edna took a step back, and her foot crunched down from the icy snow. Only this time her foot didn't stop. It kept going down until it plunged into the freezing water below. Hugh caught her arms and hauled her back toward the forest, but her boot was soaked. She lifted her skirt so she could survey the battered item. It had been through their rainy, muddy hike, dried by a trapper's stove, and was now wet through once more. Should she toss it in the river now? It was of little use to her dripping.

"That was close." Hugh frowned at her damp boot.

Edna glared up at Hugh. "*You* were too close. You pressed me backward."

Hugh laughed. "I didn't press you anywhere. You stepped backward."

He moved between her and the horse, ready to help her into the saddle. Her boot squelched with each step toward Pete's horse, and the once-cold water was slowly becoming warm inside her boot. She knew it wouldn't stay warm for long. The remainder of the ride would be most uncomfortable. She climbed into the saddle with a final gush of water and leaned over to watch water dribble, surprised to find it wasn't hanging down like an icicle. She sucked in a sharp breath. *Frostbite.*

But Hugh was at her wet boot, working the buttons through the holes.

"How do you do this every day?" he muttered, struggling with a button.

"Well, the holes are smaller ever since we hiked through the wet to get to Pete's."

"But you've buttoned them since then."

"Yes, well, I think I might have thrown a few curses in the process."

Hugh stopped and looked at her with a mix of disbelief and admiration. She laughed. Sometimes when he looked at her like that… she felt like he saw her and appreciated *her*. Not her beauty, not her abilities in the kitchen, not her strength or determination, but all of her, even the weak parts.

She watched him with this new wonderment. She imagined what would it be like to be loved by someone who didn't require anything. Who allowed the other person to grow and develop at whatever pace they'd set for themselves. She shook her head, it was too foreign for her even to dream.

If she told him about Brandon, would he think her weak? And if he did find her lacking in courage, would he even mind? As she watched him work each tiny button, she was certain he wouldn't care. He was a man who was strong, strong enough to love the weak. His family must have nurtured that ability. Edna thought of Brandon, forever disappointed, forever wanting more from others. She saw now that Brandon was nothing she wanted in a husband. He never had been; he was merely familiar.

Finally, the boot fell off. Hugh shook out the water and tossed the boot to the snowy earth. Her foot was immediately shocked by the cold air. She wiggled her toes, hoping to warm them with movement. He removed his hat and the bandana he wore underneath and wrapped the gloriously warm piece of fabric around her foot.

She gave a soft moan at the heat of his bandana and his hands on her chilled foot. "You've been holding out on me."

Hugh kept his eyes on the cloth he was tying off.

"You've had this warm bit of fabric all this time. I would have liked it around my neck."

Hugh glanced at the cloth she had tied around her neck and narrowed his eyes.

Edna touched the corner of the plain blue cloth Pete had given her. "Yes, I have this, but it isn't warm. I would have liked to switch it out on occasion with your warmer one."

Hugh smiled, his bright teeth shining out from the shadow of what used to be scruff and over these last few days had turned into a full beard. "Is that what I am to you? Remover of shoes, warmer of hankies?"

He stepped away, plucking her ruined boot from the snowy ground and stuffing it into the saddle bag. With nimble hands, he adjusted her skirt so it covered her shoeless foot. Already the bandana had lost most of its warmth, but she could still remember the feel of the warm fabric on her icy, wet toes. The memory of him clung to it as well.

She scooted forward to make room for him on the saddle. "It's only fair. I was bandager of bullet wounds and fetcher of alcohol."

Hugh climbed onto the saddle and leaned into her back, his lips brushing her ear. "I didn't have *that* much alcohol." He collected the reins and tugged on one side to turn the horse around. His chest pressed against her back, and she didn't care to move away. She wanted to feel him close, if just until they reached Aster Ridge. Nothing would be the same once they arrived.

She turned her head and stared at his arm. "Thank you. For taking care of my boot and my foot. I was fearing that sickness that takes toes. What did you call it?"

"Chilblains." His voice sounded different, or perhaps it was that, this close, she could feel the rumble of it as well as hear it.

"Yes. If I'd gotten chilblains, I might have lost a few of my suitors, and I can't have that. Not when I've just learned about them."

"You knew. Women always know." His voice held a touch of bitterness.

Edna's back prickled at the change in his tone. "Of course. I forgot how much you know about my gender."

"You never waited out a single dance."

Edna wanted to toss her head, but just now she didn't want to brush against him more than was necessary. "That's because I was new. They were being gentlemanly."

"There are no gentlemen. Men are kind for a reason and nothing else."

"And why were you kind just now? Tending my foot."

"Because I was hired to transport you to Billings. I failed, but I intend to return you to Willem with all your parts still attached."

Hired. Was that all she was—a job? No. She knew better, had felt more from him. But perhaps it was the dream of the isolated cabin. Maybe he had been playing house, too, and she hadn't realized. Maybe he played it still.

"What about you? Do you think your mama will be cross with me for returning her son with a hole in his shoulder? My mama always taught me to return something better than when I borrowed it. She would be ashamed."

He gave a small laugh, his hot breath warming the fabric at the back of her neck. "My mama will be very cross. You might consider forcing me back to Pete's until it's fully healed." Hugh took her hand from the saddle horn and placed it on the rein. The sudden weight on the leather strap made the horse veer to the right.

Edna yanked her hand away. "Stop it!" she laughed.

Hugh straightened the horse, and she could almost feel his smile.

She had half a mind to take his offer and turn this horse

around, but the folks in Aster Ridge must be mad with worry. "Your mama will be glad to see you home safe. She's lost too much."

"Yes. What of your mama? Will she be worried you never arrived?"

"No." Edna gulped, trying to keep down the revived urge to tell Hugh everything. To tell him about Brandon and about how she'd never told her ma she was coming for Christmas, because she hoped she never would.

"She must have loads of faith in Willem to send you out here to him and not worry when you don't arrive on schedule."

"Willem has been good to our family." Edna hated how her silence made her mother sound like an uncaring woman when she was the opposite. Her mother could be hard, yes, but she also had the biggest heart of anyone Edna knew. She never allowed Edna to feed the waifs who roamed the Chicago streets, claiming they would hang around the shop and drive away all their customers. But Edna had seen her don a disguise and go out to feed those very same children.

Away from the bakery and unrecognizable, her mother was free to care for those little ones. Edna had often wondered what their life might have been had her father lived. It was hard to imagine them without the bakery. Rather, she imagined them all there together, living the same life Edna knew, only with a gaggle of other siblings. As the oldest, Edna would have been like a second mother to all of them.

That dream would never be, stolen as it was by mortality. Just like Mr. Morris's mortality had stolen Hugh's dreams.

She spoke into the gray forest. "What would you do if your family was set, cared for in every way they needed? Where would you go?"

Hugh was quiet for a moment. "I would buy a place of my own. A few livestock."

"Would you keep trapping?"

His arms tightened on either side of her in a pleased way, almost like an embrace. "Yes."

"And you would marry Catherine?"

His arms loosened again, still at her sides, still touching her, but differently. Why had she asked? Why did she insist on reminding him of the girl he was meant to have? If life had been better to his family, he would be married to Catherine by now.

"I can't say."

His inability to admit it pressed at her like a pin in an unfinished dress. "It's cruel to entertain a girl, to hold her heart, when you know you don't care for her like she cares for you."

"She knows."

Edna turned, trying to see his face.

He chuckled and she turned back, resigned to the fact that she couldn't look at his face while sitting directly in front of him.

"I told her a few years back. Everyone knew Fay wasn't going to marry. She wanted to know if I was of the same position. I told her I was."

"You didn't say you wouldn't *ever* marry. Remember? We decided a nice homely girl with no family would do."

Hugh laughed, his breath warming Edna's neck.

She wanted to continue, to ask him if a nice girl from a bakery would ever do, but she swallowed her words. He'd denied Catherine all these years. There was no reason for him to change his mind when it came to Edna.

20

HUGH WANTED to pull her to him again. He'd said the wrong thing, but he wouldn't lie. Not to her. Not about Catherine. He'd be lying if he claimed he wouldn't be married to Catherine if his family life had been different. He probably would have married her years ago, perhaps at the same time Jimmy had married his sweetheart. Would he have been with Jimmy on that fateful day? Would he have saved his friend, or gone down with him?

He pushed the dark thoughts from his mind, clutching the reins tighter as Como's hooves crunched along the snowy path. Just as Edna's boot had crunched down and into the water. He replayed the moment in his mind. He'd been about to kiss her. As he'd brushed the snow from her shoulders, a desperation had surged in him. He didn't want to go home; he wanted to continue protecting her and letting her tend him in return.

In that moment, with snow dusting her collar he'd been in a trance, disappointed that he'd never kissed her in their days alone together. Now his chance had drawn to an end. A kiss would change everything. He would lose Edna's friendship the same way he'd lost Catherine's. The relationship would no longer be innocent, but hanging over the precipice of a romantic entanglement. And Hugh would once again be the villain. She was like some cascading waterfall. Beautiful and treacherous. If he got too close, he might fall over the edge, and he would never recover.

Her fall had saved him. At least they hadn't crossed a line they could not return from. Instead of kissing her lips, he'd tended her foot. After a time, they might both wonder if they really felt what they remembered. When enough time had passed, they would forget the scene altogether. Even these past few days at Pete's would be a distant memory.

The sun had nearly touched the horizon when they dropped down into their valley. His family home stood at the mouth, a thin trail of smoke rising from the chimney. He could picture his pa inside with a blanket around his legs. Mama would be in the kitchen, like usual. Fay would be at the Grahams, or perhaps she was leaving early these days with nobody to escort her in the dark.

"Mind if we stop at my place first? Just to let them know we're well. Then I'll take you on to the Grahams'."

"Of course." Her words were stiff, too formal. As though the sight of their valley meant the fog of their adventure had cleared away entirely, and they were fellow employees once again. They had returned to real life. Like every misty morning, the light of day burned away any mirage.

He rode Pete's horse right up to the hitching post and climbed off. He helped Edna down but found his hands refused to let her go when her feet touched the earth. He stared into her eyes, wishing for something—for so many things—to be different. His throat bobbed with the words he couldn't say.

She smiled, her eyes teasing. "Are you so cruel as to make them wait a moment longer than they have to?"

He laughed, releasing her waist and offering his arm as they went to the door. He pushed through and his mama hollered as soon as she saw him. She hugged him, then Edna, kissing them both on the cheeks. "We were so worried!" She surveyed them both. "Are you both well? Where have you *been?*"

Even Lachlan came in for a hug, and his eyes shined brighter, as though this spell had been shorter and was already nearly over.

"Well enough." Hugh thought of Edna's joke about returning him with a hole and gave her a conspiratorial look. "We were at Pete's."

Mama lifted to her toes to look over Hugh's shoulder. "Oh, that is a relief. Where is Fay, then?"

Hugh snapped his gaze to Mama. "Fay?"

Mama still searched outside, focused on getting the answer she expected.

Hugh gripped her arms. "Fay isn't here?"

Lachlan shuffled his feet. The movement, though small, required effort that Lachlan didn't have. He panted as he spoke. "She went looking for you. Said she was headed to Pete's."

Hugh shook his head. "We didn't see her."

Mama stepped closer. "What's that around your neck? Are you hurt?"

Hugh ignored the question, with eyes only for Lachlan. "We need to find her. There are bandits out in those woods looking for me and Edna."

Lachlan gave a hearty nod, but Mama stepped between the brothers. "You'll be going nowhere tonight. Fay is with Garrick, and I've heard stories from Della. The boy is a hand with a firearm as well as with his fists. Fay is safe enough. I'll not have one more child gallivanting through those woods, only to miss paths with the one they're searching for. We'll give her a day and then we can worry."

Hugh buttoned his lips against all the arguments he wanted to throw her way.

Mama stepped back and took Edna's elbow. "Let me get you two some grub." Mama moved her toward the kitchen.

"We have to get Edna to the Grahams," Hugh said, pinching the bridge of his nose. He didn't want to argue with his mama, but he wouldn't rest well until Fay was back here, safe.

Mama threw her hands up. "Of course you've got to get back. They'll all be so worried. Your family came all the way from Chicago to ensure your safety."

Hugh felt Edna tense at his side. He reached a hand out and placed it at the small of her back.

Edna leaned closer, cocking her head. "My mama is here?"

Ma gave Edna a warm smile. "I bet she'll be right pleased to see you safe."

Edna gave a nervous laugh. Hugh watched, looking for clues. He still hadn't sorted what was wrong with Edna's relationship with her mama. She looked both relieved and disappointed to hear the woman was in town.

Hugh spread his fingers on her back. "You're not so cruel as to make your mama wait." He smiled, hoping a tease might settle whatever fears she wrestled.

Edna looked up and grimaced. Hugh had seen enough genuine smiles these last few days that he could tell this one was forced. She nodded, and they both set off for the horse. Lachlan followed them out.

Hugh turned to his brother. "Are you well enough to feed Pete's horse? He's done a fine job carrying both of us all day. I'll take Lady."

"Fay's got her."

Hugh shook his head. "Of course. We'll take Como, and you and I can sort out what to do about Fay when I get back."

Edna teetered at Hugh's side, and he remembered she had one shoe on and the other in the saddlebag. He turned to her. "Let's get you settled." He led her to the horse, and she climbed up. He fixed her skirt to cover her wrapped foot and took the reins.

"I can take myself." Edna reached out, palm up, waiting for him to pass her the reins. "You've got enough to worry about here."

Hugh shook his head. He would see her home safe and face whatever lashing Willem saw fit to give.

He led the horse down the path, his worry for Fay tipping between certainty that both parties had been quiet enough to miss one another along the path and fear that she'd come across the same bandits he had. When they got to Bastien and Della's house, he walked the horse right to the front door and knocked. Then he stepped to the horse's side and lifted Edna down. He kept an arm around her waist, letting her lean on him so her wrapped foot didn't have to touch the cold ground.

"Sorry." He looked down at her. "About your boot. I should have given you more space when we were in the forest. I'll get it." He let her go, allowing her to lean on the doorframe before he stepped away.

He'd just opened the saddle bag when the door opened and warm yellow light spilled out.

"Edna," Bastien breathed. He called over his shoulder. "She's here. Edna's here."

Hugh came back with the damp and half-frozen shoe in his hand. He passed it to Edna, who gave him a sweet smile. Bastien slapped him on the back. "Can I take your horse?"

Hugh glanced at Como. The beast was no doubt

exhausted, and a bit of the Grahams' quality grain wouldn't go amiss. With a grateful nod, he passed Bastien the reins.

Willem appeared in the doorway with a laugh. He wrapped one arm around Edna's shoulders and gave her a squeeze, then pushed her inside. "Go see to your mama. She's worried sick."

Willem clapped Hugh on the shoulder. "Glad you're both safe."

Hugh swallowed, his stomach turning with regret. "I lost the coach and the team. Made Pete Corbin a few enemies too." He shook his head. What a mess he'd made, all to deliver a woman who didn't want to go home in the first place. He met Willem's stare, ready to accept his consequence.

"I admit I'll miss the coach, but I hope you didn't risk your life for it. I can buy a new coach. Your family needs you around."

Hugh nodded. He didn't need the reminder—or perhaps he did. Perhaps he'd spent too much time with Edna, alone, living like neither of them had any other cares or responsibilities.

Bastien returned. "We'll take care of the horse. D'you want to step inside for a bit?"

Willem shot Bastien a look and gave a slight shake of his head. Hugh lowered his brows, looking between the two men. He hadn't a mind to go inside, but the way they spoke to each other with only their eyes told him something he'd missed.

Willem faced him again, and Hugh must have had a curious expression. Willem winced, "It's just... Edna's man is in there, brought her mama from Chicago, and I'd hate for her to face any trouble, you know?"

Her *man*? Hugh's thoughts swirled, and no matter how he tried, none of them made enough sense to be turned into words. She'd mentioned a beau, but her words had made it sound like he was in the past. Yet, if he was here, Hugh realized that spoke louder than Edna's vague words on the matter. If she had a man in the city, why hadn't she wanted to go home to him and her mother?

Through his confusion, Hugh understood Willem's hesitation. Edna and himself had both acknowledged the fact that her reputation would be in shambles if anyone knew Pete wasn't at his cabin with them during their stay. It might still be in question either way. But for her beau to hear those rumors, to see Hugh upon Edna's arrival, it would stir up trouble all right.

A cruel part of Hugh wanted to stomp right into that house, chest puffed and fists ready. *Her man.* This man had let Edna leave Chicago and come to this lawless state. Hugh wanted this *man* to see just who Edna had spent the last several days with. See if he dared question Edna's honor. See, if it came to it, whether Hugh could beat the man in a fight.

21

EDNA SAT on the bench along the entry wall and removed her one boot. She'd barely tugged it off when her mother came around the corner.

"Mama." Edna's voice cracked as she stood, dropping the boot, and wrapped her arms around her mother's stout form.

"You're alive." Her mother breathed into Edna's hair.

"I'm sorry I gave you a fright. How did you come—who's at the shop?" The questions poured from her. Edna knew better than anyone how the bakery couldn't be neglected. How their posh customers raged if every pastry wasn't made just right.

Her mother stepped back and surveyed Edna from her hair to the hem of her skirt. "We came by train, of course. Lydia wrote and said your companion was missing, and if you weren't with me, you were missing as well."

But Edna's mind snagged on one word. "We?"

"Brandon is with me."

Edna shot a look at the door as though Hugh was going to step through at any moment. She turned back to her mama and hissed, "What? Why?"

Mama leaned close and matched Edna's tone. "Gertie was with me when I received the wire."

That was enough explanation. Gertie was a gossip and thrived on being the one to deliver news. No doubt the whole street knew Edna had been missing. Of course, that meant Brandon too. And also Frederick. "Has Frederick been around?" Maybe he had given Mama a letter to deliver to Edna.

"Frederick?" Mama made a face. "No. I think Brandon did a thorough job of warning him off you."

Edna colored. She didn't realize her mother knew about that.

The click of wooden boot heels drew both their gaze, and Brandon darkened the hallway.

He wore a suit and tie, which wasn't odd for him, but after so many months away from the city his dress felt formal, almost prideful. His slicked hair, which had been stylish in Chicago, looked vain out here, where men usually covered their hair with a hat and ran their hands through it when it needed a comb.

"Edna." He said her name like honey on a spoon, thick and sweet.

"Brandon," Edna said, keeping one arm around her mother's waist like an anchor in a storm. "Thank you for accompanying my mama."

"Of course. I wanted to be sure you were safe."

Edna nodded. "I'm right as rain. We experienced a bit of a problem and had to stay on with a friend of..." her words stuck in her throat, "... mine." Pete wasn't *her* friend, but the idea of saying Hugh's name right now didn't feel right. She didn't know whether Hugh had gone home or was going to step through that door at any moment. Her heart hammered at the prospect.

The last thing she wanted was a replay of Frederick and

Brandon's encounter. Especially in front of the Grahams, who had given her a fresh start, a chance to forget all that humiliation. She glanced at Brandon. He looked smaller now, too. For once, he might finally be on the losing end of his battle to keep all men away from Edna. She couldn't say why. Was it because she remembered her hand in Hugh's and knew it was bigger, knew he would best Brandon in any battle of fists? Or was it her that had changed? That no matter the outcome, she wouldn't walk away at Brandon's side.

Brandon stepped forward and pulled Edna out of her mama's arm and into an embrace. "We prayed every day for your safe arrival."

Edna stood stiff in his embrace. *We.* Like he was her family. But she had no brothers. This man wasn't family. He was something else entirely.

The door behind her opened, and Edna pushed away to see who entered. Brandon kept a hand on her waist as Bastien stepped into the house, followed by Willem. Edna stretched her neck, but nobody followed. Relief and disappointment flooded her at the same time.

Bastien smiled at the trio in the entry. "Glad to see you found each other once more. Shall we?" He gestured toward the kitchen, and Edna was grateful for the excuse to fully break away from Brandon.

She entered what could only be described as a fray. Lydia and Della were there, pulling her in for hugs. Even Ivete and Thomas sat at the table next to Mel and Christian.

"I'm sorry to have troubled everyone so."

Ivete smiled. "*We* only came down the valley." She glanced at Edna's mama and Brandon. No doubt Ivete was dying to hear who Brandon was and why Edna hadn't mentioned him.

A wide yawn overtook Edna. Della, ever the matriarch,

bustled Edna and her mama down the hall. "The questions will keep until morning. I'll bring you a bit of water to freshen up. Then you get some rest."

ONCE THE DOOR CLOSED, Edna turned to face her mama. She spoke in a whisper. "I can't believe you brought him here." Her voice held an unintended note of irritation.

Her mama tossed her hands. "He insisted. I couldn't very well tell the ticket master to refuse Brandon's payment. But I will say he's been a gentleman, helping me get from Billings to Aster Ridge. I knew little about coming this far west."

"It isn't like home."

"It most certainly isn't. It was a mistake to send you here. I want you in Chicago, where your life isn't at risk."

Edna untucked her blouse and worked the buttons through the holes. "Mama, I'm fine. I was always fine. It's different out here, sure, but I was never in real danger." Maybe that was a falsehood, but she recalled the lightning-fast way Hugh had pulled the gun from her belt, the way he'd used his palm to pull back the hammer and shoot several times at those awful men. She didn't doubt there was danger, but with Hugh she had always been safe. Without him, something dark and hollow gaped inside her belly. Not fear, like when she'd been forced to hug Brandon. It was more the feeling that something was being lost, turned to ice. Once frozen, it would blacken and fall off, gone forever.

With a long, drawn breath she removed her shirt. She crumpled it into a ball and pressed her hands into the material. Nothing was *missing*. She couldn't have gotten so used to Hugh in just a few days. She'd be fine once she got back into the rhythm of work here at Aster Ridge. She'd made it home without frostbite; the danger was gone. So why did she feel like cold wasn't the only force which possessed the ability to consume bits of a person?

Her mother undressed as well, and she spoke as she did so. "I need you back at the shop. Sylvie isn't working out. She doesn't know a lick about hard work, and she is too addled to watch the pastries in the oven."

Edna looked at her mama with a suspicious glint. "Sylvie is great. Perhaps someone is being too harsh of a taskmaster." The girl had been helping in Mama's shop for years before they'd hired her to be Edna's full-time replacement.

Mama shot Edna a glare, and Edna laughed. She held her dress against her stomach. "I missed you."

Her mama clicked her tongue. "Then come back."

Della knocked softly and entered with an ewer and a dish. She exited just as silently with a smile for Edna.

Edna used the warm water to wash the grime from her face and neck. Then she slipped on a clean nightgown and climbed into the bed. As the covers settled on her, she sighed with comfort, a feeling of safety sliding over her. The west *was* wild, but it contained pieces of heaven. She didn't want Chicago. She wanted Montana.

She didn't want Brandon.

She rubbed her feet together, her one foot still wrapped in Hugh's handkerchief. She wanted Hugh. But Hugh didn't want her. He didn't want anyone.

Mama turned down the lantern and climbed into the bed. She undid Edna's braid and ran her thick fingers through Edna's hair the way she used to when Edna was young. With every stroke, Edna felt her mother's love. This was enough, wasn't it? Why had she ever felt she needed Brandon's love too? "Tell me about Papa."

Mama gave a contented hum. "He was a rebel." She started, the way she always did and Edna's heavy heart eased at the nostalgia. "His pa was a mason. Strong man. Strong-headed too. When your pa told them he wanted me to be his wife, your pa's folks did not approve. Soon though, they realized that was the better half of his plan. For he didn't want to stop at marrying me. We were going to *America*. Where a man could be whatever he wanted—except a king."

Edna sighed. She loved her parents' story. She could imagine her papa in far off Sweden, young and strong, facing his parents' disapproval. "And your parents?"

Mama chuckled. "My pa had hoped for me to win Johan's heart. He knew I would suffer because of his parents' disapproval, but that was the only way over there. Marry up or marry down. There was nothing else."

Edna reached up to touch her mama's hand. "Papa didn't marry down."

Mama squeezed Edna's hand. "America was everything we thought. He worked as a stone mason, but when you came along, we needed a bit more. I started selling goods, and soon I was on my feet all day, making bread and pastries. Papa kept telling me to slow down, that I didn't need to sell so much. Perhaps he was right. But *I* needed it." She said the word with such conviction, like baking bread was her calling.

Edna smiled, leaning over to turn down the lantern.

"I'm glad I kept my customers, because when your dear papa left us, they were what kept us in walls and a roof."

Edna's heart always hurt to think of her mama, so alone during those days. She had vague memories of the gray walls of their apartment before Willem had helped Mama buy the bakery. There was so little joy to remember in that place that Edna figured she must have let most of the memories slip away entirely.

Edna sighed. "America doesn't work for everyone."

Mama's hands stilled, and Edna listened to her breathing. "No, it does not. We wanted to believe that hard work was all we needed, but life is made up of much more."

"The man who brought me here?"

"Hugh." Mama confirmed his name in a way that Edna knew Hugh's name had been spoken during the time they'd been missing.

"His family is not well. His pa is worse than dead."

"Don't you say that." Mama's voice fell firm. "If a family is starving, do they kill the oldest child because they eat the most?"

"Of course not." Edna hardly understood the comparison. She'd not suggested murder.

"A family is more than money. I fear I've not taught you that. You had no siblings, nothing but me and our shop. But I would give everything to have your pa in my bed again."

The thickness in her mama's voice caused tears to prick at Edna's eyes.

"Go to sleep, my little one."

Edna closed her eyes and slowed her breathing. Perhaps this was what Hugh meant about Catherine. Perhaps nobody understood what it was to have a cripple for a father, to love someone who was the source of so much of your strife. To not be able to hope for anything more, because hoping meant losing him.

22

EDNA WOKE before her mama and studied her face. Her mama had always been fuller than most women. Her plump face bore far less wrinkles than other women her age. Mama had always told Edna she resembled her auntie on her papa's side, but Edna hoped she resembled her mama in ingenuity. In grit and determination. For Hugh's family situation had to have a remedy. Edna would enlist her mama's help to figure it out.

When Mama woke, they dressed together and left for the kitchen. Mama had been using all of Della's flour stores to soothe her worries. Now that Edna had returned home, all that was left to do was toast the bread and smear it with butter.

Edna fed the fire and they both sat close, feeling its warmth on their knees. "I want to help Hugh find freedom."

Mama nodded slowly, staring into the flames. "Could you be in trouble?" Mama glanced at Edna's stomach.

Edna scoffed at the insinuation, embarrassment warming her face. "Mama, no!"

Mama raised her brows and drew back a little. "You spent three nights with each other. It's a valid query. If he's not more to you, what business is it of yours if he is free from his family? You"—she pointed her butter knife at Edna—"are not his family."

"I just thought… well *you* did it. I hoped we could figure out a way for them to do it too."

"Are they terribly unhappy?"

Edna scowled at the fire. "I don't think unhappy is the right word. But they are struggling."

"I struggled."

"But you found your way. They have not."

"Perhaps they are not ready."

Edna wanted to grumble. Mama just didn't understand. She hadn't watched Fay and Hugh reject every selfish thing for the sake of their family. "Their eldest daughter married a man for money to pay for her brother's medicine."

Mama just bobbed her head. "I've known many to marry for money. Even I didn't marry your papa just for his handsome face."

Edna shook her head, countering the comparison. "But their sister didn't love him." Edna took a bite of her bread. Her mama made it sound like marrying for only money was perfectly acceptable.

"Brandon has a ring." Her mother's words sucked the air from the room.

Edna turned to Mama, but her round face stared into the fire.

Mama spoke to the flames. "Will you accept it?"

"Of course not."

Mama glanced at Edna, surveying her whole form like a bundle of onions at the market. "Oh? You sound certain."

"I am, Mama. I left for a reason."

"Did you?"

"If you think the only reason I left was because you urged me to do it—"

"I believe I did more than urge."

"I didn't tell Brandon my departure date."

Mama nodded. "True. Perhaps you are more mature than I believed."

Was it so immature to want the love of a man? Of course her mama would think so. "Why did you never marry again?"

Her mother stuck her lips out as she considered the question. "At first, there was no time. I had a young daughter who demanded all my energy."

Edna smirked. "You mean you had a young bakery that demanded all your energy."

Mama laughed. "Yes, and then when my daughter and my bakery were older, I suppose I didn't want to give either of them over to a man. I was used to being on my own. Answering to no man, to sleeping in my own bed with nobody to steal the covers."

A week ago, Edna might have believed this story. She'd even argued for it with Hugh, but she only liked this idea in theory. When it came to those she loved carrying the idea out, it left a sour taste in her mouth.

Everything was different now. She'd slept next to the man and knew that, while covers might shift, he also offered a warmth that had nothing to do with quilts and batting.

⸻

HUGH ROSE EARLY and walked to the Grahams to fetch Pete's horse. He glared at the house as he walked past, no doubt sheltering the man who held Edna's heart. It wasn't fair for Hugh to be jealous. Before they'd left for Billings, Edna had given Hugh no cause to believe she felt anything for him. They'd been two employees serving the Graham family; friends, perhaps, but nothing more.

Except things had changed while they'd been at Pete's. At least they had for him. But she would rather wet her boot in the creek than let him closer than necessary.

He rode the horse back home and hitched it to the post outside the door. He was going to find Fay today.

"Oh no, you aren't." His mama set her feet. "We aren't going to find anyone without the Lord on our side."

Hugh clenched his jaw. "Mama, the ox is in the mire."

"Fay has been to Pete's house more than once, and she's got Garrick with her."

Hugh lowered his brows. Mama had never been to Pete's. She knew nothing about getting there and back. If she was confident, it was because Lachlan was feeding her assurances.

"Garrick isn't familiar with these woods. Best case, she has a companion but not a guide."

"I have faith."

Hugh nearly growled with frustration. "I'll go to services, but I'm setting off after."

Mama pursed her lips, but didn't argue.

When they arrived at the meetinghouse, Hugh wished he hadn't come. Edna was there with a short, round woman who must be her mama on one side, and a well-dressed man with dark hair on her other side.

Hugh refused to meet Edna's gaze, if her eyes were even looking for him. It was entirely possible she had eyes for only one man in that chapel, and it wasn't the pastor. Nor was it Hugh. It was the man who had come with Mrs. Archer over a thousand miles to ensure Edna's safety. A man who had a history with Edna and, by the look of his fine clothing, a future.

EDNA LOOKED for Hugh after services were over. She spotted Mrs. Morris, but none of her children were with her. Edna looked among the wagons and spotted the Morrises wagon. Leaning against the buckboard was Hugh's tall frame and, walking toward him, Catherine.

She was dressed in a mint green dress, spread full with ruffles of gathered fabric. Gorgeous, as if she'd sewn a new dress just to welcome Hugh home. Catherine smiled, her big, bright teeth flashing even from this distance. She flung her arms around Hugh's neck, and his arms found their way around her waist. Edna watched the pair, feeling a blackened piece of her heart break off and slide heavy into her belly. Frostbite.

Catherine and Hugh broke apart and Hugh smiled wide as he spoke to her. Just then Catherine paused and looked over her shoulder, right at Edna, then turned back and placed a hand on Hugh's chest.

Edna turned away, her cheeks burning.

That was Hugh's future. It had always been Catherine. Edna had even known it. Fay told Edna the first week Edna had been in Aster Ridge. Nobody had hidden it from her, not like Edna had hidden Brandon from everyone.

As if her thought had dredged him up, Brandon appeared. The whole morning he'd never been far from her, his hand constantly finding the curve in her back. He was as bad as an alley cat marking his territory. She didn't doubt even during the prayer he was glaring around the room, daring any man to so much as open one eye to look upon Edna.

When he took her hand, she relented. Not because she wanted his touch, but because he would only draw others' attention if she refused him. The last thing she wanted was a scene in the churchyard. The rest piled into the Grahams' wagon, and as soon as they were out of sight of the church-goers, as soon as Brandon didn't feel the need to claim her as his, she slid her hand from his grasp, pulling little Joshua into her lap.

She stared at Brandon's hands, callused but so different from Hugh's hands. Brandon's affection brought to mind the times he was apologizing, trying to make up for some wrong he'd done. A cruel word or an embarrassing display of jealousy.

When they unloaded from the wagon at the ranch, Brandon whispered, "May I have a word with you?"

Edna's stomach clenched. She had an idea what type of word he wanted. She longed to look to her mama for help, but she kept her gaze on Brandon. She was grown now, and she couldn't expect Mama to get her out of scrapes. With effort, she forced her mouth to spread in a smile. "You are doing so now."

He didn't laugh. "Alone."

Edna swallowed. "Of course." He'd come all this way. The least she could do was give him an audience.

He led her to the barn and out of the icy wind. The familiar smell and the horses' nickering offered her no comfort.

"Edna..." he began, and he patted at his pockets as though he was missing something.

"Brandon. I'm not going back to Chicago."

He froze. His face darkened.

"I'm staying here."

"Not in this lawless country. You aren't safe—nobody is."

"I'm not returning." Edna didn't know how to say it more clearly.

"Your mama needs you at the shop."

"She'll sort it out."

"Don't be selfish. Your mother needs you. I need you."
With a flourish, he presented a ring held between his thumb
and first finger. It was gold, and even had a diamond set in
prongs at the top. "I want you to come home. Be my wife."

Edna surveyed the piece of jewelry as though a stranger
merely showed her a ring he'd bought for someone else.

He reached for her hand, but Edna stepped backward.

Brandon let his hand drop and his mouth slanted. "You're
refusing me?"

Edna couldn't fault his incredulity. She knew few people
who would believe her refusal, least of all Brandon. Last he
knew, the only way she could deny him was to sneak away in
the early morning. Now he was here, and somehow she'd
gained the ability to refuse him in person.

"I don't want to marry you."

He snatched her hand and jammed the ring on.

"Ow!" Edna tried to pull her hand back, but Brandon held
firm and tugged her close, slamming her into his chest. One
hand held her wrist and the other hooked like a vice behind
her lower back.

"Quit. Being. Selfish," he growled between clenched teeth.

He rarely handled her like this. Most of the time, the pain
he inflicted was only with words, unless he felt threatened by
somebody. The idea flickered to life in her mind. How much
did he know about who her companion had been? Had that
been why he had been scanning the congregation? Did they
tell Brandon that Hugh was a healthy young man whose
family Edna adored? A man she had started to adore?

Though her wrist pinched in his firm grip, Edna didn't
cower. "I don't love you anymore." She tried to push against
him.

"Like hell you don't." Brandon crushed his lips to hers.

Edna had little choice in the matter, but she didn't care.

Even with his lips to hers, she felt only apathy. He broke off the kiss and smirked. He kissed her again, softer this time, as though her acquiescence had removed a layer of the anger that sheathed him. "We leave tomorrow morning."

He kept hold of her wrist, his fingers pressing bruises into the skin that would blossom purple by the morning. She focused on the pain as he tugged her, stumbling, to the house. They entered the kitchen, and he held her hand aloft for all to see. "Edna has agreed to be my wife."

Edna glanced around the room, at the faces who had loved and embraced her over the past months. Brandon's flapping lips meant Edna had two choices. Allow them to believe Brandon's words, or let them experience one of Brandon's fits of temper.

She gulped, unwilling to contradict him in front of all these folks. Unwilling to let them see who she used to be—a woman tied to such a man. She would talk to him later, when nobody was around. She'd lost her voice in that barn, but she would find it again.

Della tutted and congratulated her. She asked to see the ring, but when she ambled closer Della's brows pinched with concern. Edna tried to smile. Whether Della believed her or knew now wasn't the time, she said, "the ring is beautiful," and released Edna's hand.

Lydia came in from the back rooms. Edna did better this time of pretending joy. She felt like a ghost, moving through the motions. Accepting hugs and holding her hand up, the one finger slightly higher than the rest of her hand. It was odd how easy it was to move through life without feeling. She was sickened by the ease with which she slipped into her old self. Allowing Brandon to control her with fear. She suddenly felt certain that was what Brandon's mother did. Acquiesced, allowed Mr. Clareview to do as he wished, and didn't make a fuss.

The Bible taught a woman to submit to her husband, to prevent contention, but Edna knew this wasn't what the good Lord meant, for he also said a man should cleave unto his wife. He wanted unity, not superiority.

Mama came down the hallway and froze. Edna excused herself and breezed past her mama into her bedroom. She tugged the ring from her finger and threw it onto the bed. Small as it was, it took up plenty of space on the star quilt. Mama appeared in the doorway, shutting it softly behind her.

"I'll not marry him," Edna hissed.

Mama nodded, but kept her lips sealed.

"I never agreed. He rolled me over, and he knows it." Edna closed her eyes, but the image of Catherine flaunting her relationship with Hugh flashed behind her eyelids, and Edna opened them again.

"Why do I fall for the wrong man?"

Mama stepped closer and wiped a tear from Edna's cheek. "Not every man is going to be the right one."

"And what if the right one is already taken?"

Mama drew in a deep breath and let it out slowly. "Well, then you best keep busy until another one comes along."

Edna sniffed. She didn't want another one. "I don't want to go back," she whispered, her voice thick with bottled up emotion.

Mama nodded. "Can you bear to watch him love another?" A flash of pain crossed her mama's face.

Edna knew they were talking about Hugh, but she sensed experience in her mother's words. She'd been a fool to think love was only for the young. Women remarried all the time at every age.

Edna touched her mama's arm. "Mama, who? When?" Was it before or after her papa?

Mama shook her head. "This isn't about me, dear. You

need to decide if you can live without him and, what's more, can you *live* within sight of him?"

Hugh and Catherine down the road. But, of course, when they got married, they wouldn't live in his parents' house. They would build something in town. She thought of Hugh's words, that he would buy a farm of his own. Would he be happy in town?

"So long as he was happy, I think I could."

Mama nodded, patting Edna's arm. "Willem says the train station in Billings has a ticket for you. You come home anytime."

Edna's throat felt thick. Her mama was going home tomorrow. Without Edna. She never got this much attention from her mama at home. Always the bakery, always the books. So much to worry about. "You don't need me there?"

Mama shook her head. "I want you there, more than you know. But you're a grown woman. It's time you lived your own dreams, not mine."

Edna wrapped her arms around the woman who had given her life. "I'm blessed to have a mama like you."

"You surely are. Now, are you going to go tell that man before he looks more the fool than he already does?" She lifted her chin in a mock prideful impression of Brandon.

"Has he always been so bad?"

"You never noticed before. I shouldn't be surprised you haven't noticed this time."

"He rarely lets me get far away enough to look at more than the stubble on his chin." Perhaps that was all the reason Edna needed for coming out to Montana—a little change in perspective, the ability to look around her without anyone's ideas pressing upon her mind.

"Brandon will be far enough away for you to keep seeing him for what he is. Can you go to your friend Fay's house until we leave in the morning?"

"I won't run away again, Mama. That...wasn't good for me. I need to face him. So there's no confusion for him or for me." For she'd been running away from more than Brandon. She had been running from herself, from her own cowardice, and she would not do so again.

23

LUCKILY, Edna only had to dry her tears once. Due to Garrick's safe arrival, as well as news that Fay too was home safe, the Graham household was bursting with the excitement of a rushed Christmas feast before the wagon left tomorrow morning to take passengers to Billings. There was plenty of work to be done in the kitchen, and as always, Edna found herself submersed in the task. Edna recognized the tactic from her years in Chicago, pressing her frustrations into a batch of dough, rolling it into paper thin layers. Perhaps the reason Mama's help was falling behind was because Sylvie had a balance in her life and never a need to furiously work to scrub her mind of the man she'd let into her heart.

Edna suppressed the memory of the woman she'd been. She would embrace the familiar feeling of being in the kitchen with her mother by her side and an insurmountable task ahead. "Is Sylvie really struggling?"

Mama lifted a shoulder. "She does well enough, but she's no Archer."

"I don't suppose you want to set up shop in Dragonfly Creek? I think you'll have at least ten customers."

Della bumped Edna with her hip. "That's just in town. You're not counting all of us. Heaven knows Willem would find time every day to make the drive and pick us all up our share."

Mama laughed. "You don't need me when you've got an Archer all to yourself right here."

"But she's not staying."

Edna fell silent. The men were at the fireplace, but still within earshot, and Edna could almost see Brandon's ears twitch, like a wolf listening for weakness.

When Edna met Della's eyes again, Della gave a slow nod of understanding. How much she understood, Edna wasn't sure. But Della had seen Edna's glance toward Brandon, and she'd not missed Edna's struggle to feign happiness at Brandon's engagement announcement.

Edna looked around the kitchen at the women and realized she'd missed out on having sisters, but she had a type of sisterhood right here. These women were close, they were loving, they were perceptive. If she wasn't going to be in Chicago with her mama, Edna didn't want to be anywhere but right here.

HUGH SAT ON THE HEARTH, letting the fire warm his back. His wound didn't bother him much. The herbs Pete had shared must have done their job in chasing away the blood poison. Edna flashed into his mind, uninvited, and he opened his mouth to ask his sister for advice.

Just then, a soft knock sounded. Hugh glanced at Fay, whose wide eyes told him whoever knocked remained a mystery to her as well.

Hugh opened the door to find Garrick on the other side. "Thought you could use a bit of this bread. Apparently, Edna's mama is a baker."

Hugh almost laughed. It was hard to remember that Garrick hadn't been around for a few years. He fit so seamlessly into life at Aster Ridge.

"Edna shares the talent, but apparently not the compulsion to bake at all times."

"I think it was a way to soothe her nerves. But I guess there was no need. She's safe, as are you, and headed back to Chicago with her mother and soon to be wed."

"Wed?" Hugh's heart tumbled down his chest, like a shoe hitting every hollow step down the porch stairs.

"He's her fiancé now, got engaged earlier today."

Hugh's throat grew thick, nearly choking him as he tried to swallow the lump away. "Good for her." The words stung as bad as Pete's moonshine, and the news was just as hard to ingest.

Logic told him this was good for her. That man he'd seen at the chapel was the type of man to make any girl happy. Edna hadn't looked overly happy today, like a woman newly engaged, but surely one wasn't expected to smile at all times. Had she been engaged when he'd seen her? Or had it happened after church? His mind snagged on this question, though he knew it didn't matter. Engaged was engaged. Either way, there would be a wedding at the end, and such an event would take place in her hometown of Chicago.

He tried to picture her there and couldn't. Not because his emotions refused to think of her with any man other than him, but because she'd never spoken of her life in Chicago. She'd spoken of her ma, but she'd shared little else.

Hugh didn't know the least bit about Chicago Edna. He was a fool to think a few days meant he knew somebody. Those days in the woods had been a pause on life. Like he and Edna had hopped into a bedtime story and lived in a fictional world for a moment before hopping out, shutting the book, and turning out the light.

Engaged.

Garrick's eyes kept darting to Fay, but Hugh didn't possess the capacity to dive into what their shifting eyes might mean. Finally, Garrick took his leave and Hugh shut the door behind him with a resounding click. He walked back to the spot on the hearth where he'd been sitting before Garrick had arrived and shattered everything.

Fay came over and sat next to him once again. "Did you expect this?"

Hugh shook his head.

"Me neither."

They sat in the quiet of a half-asleep house, broken only by the occasional pop of the fireplace or a cough from their parents' room.

Fay leaned her elbows on her knees. "I always thought she fancied you. I never knew why she held back. I guess I do now."

He heard the hurt in Fay's voice. Betrayal.

"I'm sure she had good reason. You should see him, all glossy and neat."

Fay snorted. "Every woman's dream."

"He doesn't have to be every woman's dream. Just one." Hugh had no idea who he'd been competing with. Had he known there was *any* competition, he might have never dared dream. Seeing Brandon, that would have flattened Hugh completely. The man was rich, it was obvious. He was familiar with Edna. A little too familiar, if the way he touched her was any indication.

"You've got a look." Fay pulled him from his thoughts.

"What sort of look?"

"Like you want to kill the man."

Hugh sighed and relaxed his face. "I don't. I just...feel a fool."

"What happened? Tell me everything."

Hugh laughed. "I'm not telling *you* anything."

"Did she make you a promise? She couldn't have known Brandon was going to show up here. Maybe he's nothing to her. Maybe she doesn't know you love her."

"I *don't* love her."

"Coulda fooled me." Fay leaned back against the stone next to the fireplace.

Did he love her? He thought about her constantly. He wanted her to be happy. He wished she could be happy with him. All of those things might mean love, but they also told him to let her go. "She should marry him. Go back home, back to the life where she belongs."

"But she loves it here. She never said she was going back." Fay's face twisted in thought. "Course, she never said she had a beau either."

"I doubt her beau has any intention of staying out here." Hugh's voice sounded childish and bitter, but he didn't have the heart to correct it. Edna wasn't staying. That man of hers had every intention of resuming whatever life had bought him those clothes and a whim train ticket to Montana.

———

HUGH WOKE before the sun and started readying Pete's horse. He'd barely slept, waking easily, and every time he did, it took him a moment to remember he wasn't in Pete's cabin with Edna sleeping next to him. The reason it took so long was because as soon as the truth hit, he would close his eyes and pretend. Just for a moment, in the safety of his own bed. He would slow his breathing, and he could almost smell her, feel her hand between his shoulder blades, her breath warming his back inside a different set of walls.

Hugh loaded Pete's horse with a tall basket filled with bread. It was going to grow mold before Pete could eat it all, but Garrick swore the Grahams had plenty more.

He set off for Pete's house with an eye on the horizon. If he kept a decent pace, he would make it back in time to sleep in his own bed.

Less than an hour in, Garrick caught up to him on the road. "I'm glad you haven't turned off yet."

"You must have set off early." The last thing Hugh had expected was company.

Garrick shrugged. "The house was up early readying the wagon for the trip."

To Billings. The wagon would carry Edna and her family, both old and new. Hugh couldn't bring himself to ask for confirmation. Of course they would be headed right back. What was here for them? Edna and Willem had both mentioned how Mrs. Archer couldn't be away from the bakery. Now she'd been away for several days. But Edna would help get the business back on track. Edna wasn't afraid of hard work. She wasn't afraid of anything.

Except going home.

He couldn't shake the thought that he was missing an important detail, an explanation. Why had she left Chicago at all? Wasn't she afraid her fancy man would find himself a new woman? The cities weren't aching for women the way the west did. Here, a man might wait a year for a woman to return, partially because it was unlikely he would stumble across another willing to marry him in that year's time. Surely that wasn't the case in Chicago.

Engaged. Engaged?

His mind refused to process the thought. Instead, it lingered at the back of his throat, threatening to choke him with its unlikeliness. He doubted a hard day's ride would shake her from his thoughts, but he would do his best. With her gone, perhaps forgetting her would be a sight easier than it would have been with her working at Aster Ridge.

But even as he urged his horse faster, he knew no amount of jostling, no discipline would shake her loose. She was stuck good, and a decent bit of festering would come before he had any hope of being rid of her completely.

24

BETWEEN MAMA SHARING her bed and thoughts of what was to come this morning, Edna had hardly slept. In mere hours she would set Brandon straight and send him to Chicago without her. The question was, how would he take her revelation? Would he yell or shout? Would Edna have to rebuild the reputation she'd built here in Aster Ridge?

She almost laughed. To think Hugh had been overly concerned about what everyone thought. Maybe this was the very reason Edna hadn't cared about such traditions. She'd long ago learned there was little one could do to quell the judgment of others.

She tossed until the early morning when her mama groaned and shoved at Edna's shoulder. "Go *do* something with all that energy."

Edna dressed and milked the goats. Part of her wished they'd escaped again, run home to the Morris' yard. She looked to the east and hated her desperation. Did she think Hugh would abandon the giant amount of work he did every day and come here to beg her to stay? Why would he do such a thing? He didn't know Brandon, didn't even know Edna was engaged.

She milked the unusually well-behaved goats and brought the warm liquid into the house. In the quiet kitchen, she fried herself a bit of egg-toast and sat down in the quiet of the morning to eat.

Brandon came inside long after the rest of the household had woken. She took a breath, steeling herself for what she had to do. Weaving through the throng of men, women, and children, Edna touched his wrist. "Brandon, may I speak with you for a moment?" She glanced at the fireplace, torn between wanting privacy and wanting witnesses. In the end, she decided the quiet nook outside the front door would satisfy both.

He joined her, though the way his gaze followed the men as they readied the wagon told her he was more interested in getting on their way than in anything Edna had to say.

She took his hand and turned it over, palm up. She traced the line that ran under his calluses. The same line a gypsy had once told Edna was her love line. She wished she could see his future, see who he was going to become. He wasn't all bad. No man was. She'd seen the softer side, seen how he loathed his father's treatment of his mother. He didn't possess the clarity to see that same darkness in himself. There was good in him, but Edna wasn't the woman to bring it out. Perhaps that woman was out there, or maybe Brandon was the only one who could help himself.

She set the ring in his upturned palm. The diamond didn't shine, not in the gloomy, overcast sky.

He pinned her with his gaze, his full attention finally on her. His chest heaved with slow, intentional breaths. "I thought you didn't want to work your life away, the way your mama did."

He was right. She'd told him plenty of times how she

resented the bakery, how she hoped to be more present in her own children's lives. But she knew, now more than ever, that providing a life for a dependent was anything but easy. Anyone could say that they wanted out of the hard, laboring life, but creating an easy life was a different matter altogether. For some, like Hugh, it was impossible to get ahead.

"She did her best."

The moment Edna said it, it took root in her, and a surge of respect and love for her mama grew inside and choked her. She pressed her lips together, her chin quivering with the effort of holding back her tears.

Brandon's eyes turned sad, pleading. "Don't do this. If it pains you, come with me."

Edna shook her head, content with him misconstruing her tears for her mama as tears for him. "I'm not going back. I don't love you."

He jerked his chin up, pinning her with a scowl. "You think you're going to find better in these backwoods?"

Edna shrugged. She might not find herself a husband. "I'm content to be alone." For that's what she had learned these past months. She liked herself. Spending time alone was a joy, and if she found a man who loved her, but also didn't take that away, who added to that joy, she would count herself lucky.

Brandon snorted in a way she recognized. That familiar dip in her chest at his disrespect—shame. Disappointment. She was used to him feeling these things toward her. Only, this was the first time she felt she'd truly earned them–at least in his eyes. How disappointed he must be to find that woman he knew was gone. She was no longer pliable, no longer his to possess.

"Hate me." Edna shrugged. "Go tell them I've gone mad out here in the west. Tell them I live a sad life and I'll die a spinster." Edna chuckled, certain he would have said all these things without her permission.

Brandon's fingers curled around the ring, each knuckle turning white.

Edna looked up at him, unafraid, for his mistreatment had helped her learn something she might have never learned. She was enough. "The ring was beautiful. Thank you for offering it to me."

Brandon's nostrils flared as he glared at her. She could almost hear the things he was saying inside his head; he'd said them all plenty of times before. Dumb. Lazy. Naive. Self-ish. Desperate. Now she knew if she had been any of those things, it had been due to staying with him. Allowing him to mistreat her.

He raised his clenched fist, and Edna felt that newly familiar apathy. He could hit her, but it would be no worse than the kick she'd gotten from a goat that morning. Painful, but only on the outside, for the blows he delivered had nothing to do with her. They were the reaction of an animal who was too stunted to know better.

As he stormed away from her, she prayed he would learn that he wasn't cursed to be this same man forever.

A cold wind blew, but not the gusting kind. This was slow and touched her neck in a way that caused a shiver to run down her sides, all the way to each foot. And she smiled, for it was a comfort to know she could still feel. The numbness that had crept over her the moment Brandon had jammed that ring on her finger was dissipating. She was her own again. Nobody else's.

She stood and couldn't stop her gaze from drifting east again. This time the horizon wasn't empty. Fay's lone figure walked down the path from their house. Edna rushed to meet her and took Fay's hands. "You went after us." Her words were a lament.

"Well, technically I went for Hugh." Fay smirked and Edna hooked her arm, settling in at her friend's side as they walked to the main house.

"How is he?" She thought of his wound and chastised herself for wishing she could be the one to change his bandage every day. As they walked to the house, Edna watched the men load the wagon with more than just Brandon and Mama's things. The Grahams must be planning on a bit of a stay in Billings. She hoped they had plenty of bullets and guns.

Fay cleared her throat. "Hugh's sad about losing you."

Edna coughed and looked at Fay. "What?"

"*I'm* sad to lose you." Fay pulled Edna in for a tight embrace.

Edna blinked as Fay held her. When they broke apart, Edna cocked her head. "Who told you I was leaving?" Edna had considered this in her sleepless night, afraid someone would tell Hugh she was engaged. But none of the Grahams had gone to the Morris' because of the Christmas festivities.

"Garrick."

Ah, she'd forgotten about him. How had he slipped out of the celebration unnoticed? She wasn't yet used to having him around. Too many mouths around here, and not just to feed.

Edna gave her friend's arm a squeeze. "I wish you'd had a little more faith in me. I'm staying."

Fay looked at her sidelong. "Faith? Not sure what you expected from me. I didn't even know you had a beau."

"I don't. I did, but that was before I came."

Fay gave her a critical look. "But now he's your intended. Did you ever plan to return after Christmas?"

Edna winced at her friend's hurt and at the prospect of telling Fay what a coward Edna had been. Fay would never have ditched a man without a word. She never would have stood for the treatment Edna had. Women like her didn't understand what desperation was. Fay's desperation with her family was tangible, understandable. Edna's wasn't visible to everyone, not even really to her. She'd wrestled with it her whole life, not understanding it. How could she expect a spirited woman like Fay to comprehend?

"I was here for nine months with no word to him. If he didn't know it was over, it was because he refused to acknowledge it. I never gave him reason to believe I still loved him."

"Except when you accepted his proposal."

Edna chewed her lip, nodding. "He walks all over me, and he doesn't tread lightly."

Fay's brows drew together. "He treats you poorly?"

Edna shook her head. *Not anymore.* "He's nothing to me. Just the past."

They pushed into the house and Fay was welcomed with hugs and kisses and a bit of breakfast pushed into her hands. Edna hadn't been the only one expecting Fay to take a day to herself after traveling for two.

To avoid Brandon, Edna said goodbye to her mother inside the house. It was short, for they'd said everything last night and, as always, Mama was Edna's champion.

Soon, only Fay remained in the kitchen.

Edna turned to her. "I haven't seen Hugh this morning."

"He's off to return Pete his mount."

Edna blinked. "Today? But who is with him?"

Fay shrugged. "Nobody."

Edna's heart started to gallop in her chest. "But the bandits are looking for him. Did he learn *nothing*?"

Fay laid a hand on Edna's arm. "He's quite capable of taking care of himself. It's a coach and a lady he loves that made things difficult."

Loves?

Edna shook her head. "Hugh doesn't love me. He cares for

me as a friend, that is all." She thought of the way he'd pressed her backward when she'd soaked her foot. Perhaps there might have been more, if she'd caught him off guard, but so long as he was thinking properly, he was intent on being the man for his family.

"If he does, he's a fool. Oh," Fay reached into her pocket, "Garrick and I brought a letter for you from Dragonfly Creek."

Edna jumped, staring at Fay's pocket like it might hold the answers to every unanswered prayer. Fay laughed as she handed it over.

Edna's name was written on the envelope in Frederick's handwriting. She tore open the paper and rushed to unfold the letter.

Edna,

I'm glad to hear you are well. My family is doing fine. Selma is getting married soon. You do not know her intended, for he just came over from Sweden. His family knows our papa's family, and that is enough for us.

I'm pleased to hear from you, as well as pleased to hear you intend to help your friends out west. Please know no cure has been discovered. This is merely a remedy to be taken regularly. Enclosed is a recipe. Your friend's physician will likely suggest he consume Sappinton's Pill. I beg you to only give him the recipe I have included. Sappington's formula contains Arsenic, which will lead to death. Many physicians refuse to change their treatment. For that, I apologize on behalf of my kind. Please write if you have trouble finding any of these ingredients. I am happy to send what is needed to an old friend.

Take care and write again soon.

Best,

Frederick

Edna found another paper enclosed with ingredients, estimated prices, and dosage instructions. She clutched the letter to her chest, her smile wider than she would have thought possible. She turned, but Fay had gone. The house was empty, and Edna collapsed onto a seat, basking in something going right for once.

HUGH AND GARRICK arrived at Pete's and waited only for Garrick's mount to have a drink, then they were off again.

Once out of the dense wood surrounding Pete's cabin, Garrick came to ride at Hugh's side. "Fay says he used to be close to your family."

"Still is, as much as he can be while living out here like this."

"He's a frightening fellow. There were many like him in the Rough Riders. Here, they are washed up. There, they were warriors."

"He's not washed up from age." Hugh mourned the loss of another Corbin, but unlike Jimmy, Pete had been lost to the forest and not the ground. "Life is hard."

"It sure is. There are all kinds of hard. It seems few have it easy, and even those ones don't."

Hugh nodded at the all too accurate statement. "You still planning to join your friend in Texas?"

"I am. He's got an opportunity for me out there."

"There's opportunity here."

Garrick glared at the valley. "I'm ashamed of who I was here. I don't want to live in that memory."

Hugh surveyed Garrick. Hardly the boy he was when Eloise married Aaron. "You leave, we all live with you in that memory. Stay and you make a new name for yourself."

Garrick twisted his mouth. "The Grahams have pretty well got this valley settled. What am I going to do? I want a life of my own, not to live in the fringes of their life."

Hugh's heart weighed heavier with every step of his horse. He couldn't argue with Garrick. Some days Hugh wanted nothing more than to get away from his family, to see who he was away from the burden of their illnesses. His grip tightened on the leather reins. Surely that wasn't what Garrick meant. Surely, *he* wouldn't leave if his family needed him. But still, Hugh wished with a sickening desperation that he could trade places with Garrick. Let the man stay and be needed and Hugh would gallivant, trying to find himself in volunteer wars and half-promised possibilities.

When they reached the mouth of the valley, Hugh broke off the path, nodding goodbye to Garrick, who continued to the Graham ranch. When he stepped into the house, he stopped short. Edna was at the table with his ma and Fay, a kaleidoscope of colored fabric spread on the surface.

He blinked away the idea that he was dreaming. "I thought you were headed to Chicago."

Edna said nothing, but her throat bobbed.

Fay stood and tugged their mama out of her seat. "Come look at this fabric I've got in my room."

Hugh watched them go, guilt cutting at his gut. How had he ever wished to leave them behind, to gallivant as Garrick had done? His place was here, and he had better make his peace with that or risk going mad.

Hugh turned back to Edna. She held a needle passed partway through two small scraps of fabric. She set them down and stood, wiping her hands on her skirt. Then, as though she remembered something, she reached into her pocket and pulled out a folded paper.

"I wrote to a friend in Chicago."

Hugh nodded. *Now* she was speaking of her life in Chicago. Now that she had no choice about everyone knowing her business.

"He's an apothecary. He sent me a recipe. I showed your

mama, and she figures it will be at least half the cost of the medicine they buy from the apothecary in Billings."

Hugh stepped forward and took the offered paper. The writing slanted and scrawled across the page.

Edna chewed her cheek. "I just thought maybe things could be different for you. If you didn't have your brother to worry about so much."

"The doc said there is no cure. Just treatments."

Edna nodded at the paper. "Frederick says the same. This isn't a cure. Lachlan will still have malaria, but he'll be able to work the farm. The spells shouldn't come often, maybe not at all. He can help, always."

"Instead of me."

Edna's face folded. Maybe he had been unfair in his criticism of Catherine. Perhaps all women wanted a man without other responsibilities. Perhaps it was his duty to cure Edna of that want the way he'd tried curing Catherine.

He turned sharply away from her.

His boots thudded with each short step. "What? Did you think Lachlan's medicine was all that held me here? I've been committed to this family since before his illness. You've only taken us back to a year ago. You haven't fixed anything. I'm still saddled to this family. If you stayed here, hoping I could leave them behind, you're wrong."

Edna lifted her chin and turned away from him. She walked to the door and pulled her jacket from the peg on the wall. Such a familiar scene, one he could have grown used to. But she had fancy options for marriage and Hugh was not one of them. She considered him as nothing more than a problem she wanted to fix, but he wanted to be the *answer* to someone's prayers, not the reason for them being down on their knees. The click of the door charged the house with a sense of finality. Edna was much easier to run off than Catherine had been.

Fay came out from the hallway, a glare on her face. "You butchered that." She mirrored Edna in putting on her jacket and leaving. The door clicked again, and Hugh was glad, for he couldn't have borne the need to walk Edna safely to the ranch.

Even so, he would set off soon to walk Fay home. He closed his eyes. Would there ever be a time he wasn't needed?

He looked at the paper Edna had left behind. The recipe that would save his family money. If they'd had this sooner, Eloise might not have needed to marry Aaron. Then again, it was always something. If it wasn't this, it would be something else.

Edna wanted to help, and perhaps she had helped, but she was wrong in expecting him to abandon his family. He would have to be clear with her the way he'd been with Catherine. Tell her he never meant to marry, allow her to move away from him. She was right. His actions had spoken louder than his words. He would keep his distance from both women, truly allow them to find men who could make them happy.

The idea of Catherine doing so brought him joy, for she was someone he cared about after years of friendship. But the idea of Edna doing so...that same lump stuck in his throat. The one that he'd thought had to do with her being engaged. Perhaps it would always be there whenever he thought of Edna.

He'd been harsh with her. But had he been harsh enough for her to give up? He hoped so.

25

EDNA RUSHED FROM THE MORRIS' home and into the dark night. As she walked, small white flakes fell around her. She looked up to find they were all around, circling her, then falling to the ground and melting when they touched the too-warm grass. She wanted to fall there, too, and melt.

She'd been a fool to think Hugh a better man than Brandon. No man was better; they only doled out pain differently. She should have stuck to her plan of not falling for any man who elicited emotions. For if she didn't feel for him, her cheeks wouldn't be wet at the thought of him.

The sound of a door clicking behind her made her pick up her pace once again. She fairly ran before she heard Fay call out her name.

Edna slowed, turning to see Fay jogging toward her.

Edna's cheeks burned with embarrassment. She'd always hated when Brandon talked down to her in front of witnesses. Not because she thought they agreed with anything Brandon had said, but because there were witnesses to what she would forgive. Forgiving Brandon had been one thing. He had appreciated it, and she had longed for his love. But for another to see how little she esteemed herself...she could not abide that.

"He didn't mean it. He's sensitive when it comes to Lachlan."

"Don't." Edna cut her friend off. She'd heard *I didn't mean it* enough times from Brandon. She didn't need to hear it on Hugh's behalf from his sister.

But once Fay fell silent, Edna realized she *wanted* Fay to talk, to convince her that Hugh hadn't meant any of it. That it was all just a misunderstanding. But the venom in his voice hadn't been fake. She'd hurt him in trying to fix his family, and he'd lashed out at her in return.

When they were in sight of the main house, Fay slowed to a stop.

Edna stopped too, and looked at her friend. With every beat of Edna's heart, hurt pumped into her extremities. Manners instilled in her long ago made her want to say something, but her heartache meant she could think of nothing to push past her lips. Instead, she nodded at Fay and continued into the house.

EDNA WORKED all week with a mixture of sadness and joy. For she'd known she wanted to stay here for herself, but she hadn't expected the crushing weight she'd felt at Hugh's rejection of her help. She knew from Fay that they'd acquired the ingredients and Lachlan had taken his first dose without complaint about the cost, for mixing it themselves was far cheaper than buying the tablets premade.

She was happy to help the family, but she couldn't bear to be around Hugh. If ever she knew he was in the barn, she found something to do inside, even if it meant the clothes in the yard would wrinkle in the tub.

If she thought the week a trial, Sunday proved hellfire. Catherine Price found Edna almost as soon as she climbed down from the wagon. Catherine linked Edna's arm as though they were the best of pals. They walked along the pebbled path that circled the church.

Catherine smiled, but her voice dropped like ice. "There is a bit of talk around town. Nasty gossip about you and Hugh out at Pete Corbin's homestead."

Edna stared ahead, her lips tight.

"I don't believe any of it, of course. Hugh's told me more than once that you're practically a sister to him."

"Yes." Edna agreed. Sister enough to bicker like siblings.

"I must say, I'm glad to know you don't have your heart set on him. I thought you knew, but for a moment I wondered."

"Knew what?"

"That Hugh and I are promised."

Of course. Maybe *promised* was a generous word, but Edna understood Catherine's meaning. If Hugh was marrying anyone, it would be Catherine.

"Yes, I knew. I'm sorry you doubted."

"Well, I only doubted for a moment, and only because of the way everyone was talking. I heard Pete wasn't even there when you two were."

Panic rose in Edna's throat. Hugh said he would keep that detail to himself. They both would. But she hadn't told anyone, and that left only one person. The fact that he would reveal that…it made no sense. Maybe she didn't know Hugh at all. If he was going to run his mouth, it would be her responsibility alone to quell the rumor.

"Pete was there," she said. "The scariest host I ever met."

Catherine laughed, that high tinkling thing. Edna

glanced around. It was just the two of them. Could she really be so feminine that that laugh was genuine and not for show? Or was even this conversation a performance for her?

Catherine sighed. "Pete is absolutely mad. First his wife died when smallpox swept through the town, then Jimmy had a horrible accident. My best friend was married to Jimmy, and even *she* didn't grieve the way Pete did. She's married again, to a rich fellow who treats her right. Jimmy was always workin', never paid her any attention once they wed."

"I'm sorry for her." Edna spoke the words, but she wasn't sure if that was even Catherine's intent. Seemed as though congratulations were in order for Catherine's friend finding herself a better man all around.

"Sorry?" Catherine waved a lace-gloved hand. "She's been married twice now." Catherine leaned in. "The pity should be for *us*. We'll be old maids if we don't secure a match soon."

Edna nodded. They were nearly to the front of the church again, and Edna hoped she'd find a familiar face so she could break away from this torturous conversation.

Catherine continued. "I think your little adventure helped things along. Hugh was right pleased to see me on Sunday. But don't you worry. Soon as the men see that the gossip is just that, and of course that you're not carrying a wee Morris of your own, they'll be back at your heels. In fact, my brother might even be persuaded."

Edna grimaced. "Thank you, but I hope no man ever has to be *persuaded* on my behalf."

They reached the front and Catherine tugged Edna tighter. "Every *good* man needs a bit of persuading. It's only the ones who can't stand themselves that hurry to latch onto someone better."

She released her then, and with a wink and a dimpled

smile, Catherine joined her family as they walked up the steps into church.

Most of the families had begun filtering inside, including the Grahams. Edna found them easily, in the same bench they always shared with the Morrises. Except, since everyone had already found their seats, only one spot remained at the end—next to Hugh.

Edna had half a mind to feign an illness and wait in the cold wagon until services were over. Hugh shifted, making a smidgen of more room in a way that was meant more as a signal to sit down than to actually make any space. He met her eyes for the briefest of moments, then he looked at his hands in his lap once more.

Edna sat, her arm brushing against his. She leaned her elbow on the sloped arm of the pew, hoping to put as much distance between them as possible. Catherine filled Edna's mind like a fog, obscuring everything else. Her laugh, her words, her surety that Hugh belonged to her alone.

The meeting started with an opening hymn. Hugh's voice cut through the Catherine-fog and Edna found herself calmed by the words in the hymn. She wanted to hear the song he'd sung to her at the cabin, about the lovers. She closed her eyes, her heart too heavy to sing.

She'd strayed from her promise not to be with a man who incited too much feeling. It wasn't a bad plan, to choose her spouse with reason instead of emotion. For once the love for Brandon had gone, once the need to make him happy had evaporated, she had been able to see him for what he was, and see her future for what it might be. She had been able to reject him, and not as a coward hightailing it out of town.

Yet here sat a new man who tangled her mind with emotion, whose rejection cut at her heart and brought it low.

Edna gripped the edge of the seat and stared at the ground. Hugh's singing proved fine as ever, but it brought her no peace this day. She closed her eyes, remembering her mama's words. *Can you live seeing him with someone else?*

No, Mama. I cannot. Edna's throat felt thick, and she sniffed back her tears while there was still music to cover the sound.

26

HUGH SAT at Edna's side, anger beating through him. He thought he'd been too harsh with her last night, but then this morning she had taken a stroll with Catherine as though they were the best of friends. He'd been a fool to think a few days stranded at Pete's meant he knew her. What was more important was that he knew *women*, knew they wanted more. More than Hugh. More than surviving, they wanted to *live*. And he refused to blame them for wanting all that.

But then she pressed her hand along the edge of the bench between them and Hugh stared at it, white knuckles and tendons, pressing down as though she fought a battle with herself. Her eyes were closed, and since the meeting had just begun, he figured it wasn't the Holy Spirit coming over her. His heart reached out, and he couldn't stop his hand from doing the same.

He reached down, his pinky finger overlapping hers. He closed his eyes, too, and for a moment he pretended they were still in Pete's bed, relying on each other. He sang out in a way he never did in public, singing to her like he'd done Christmas morning.

The song ended, and he leaned over and whispered, "I'm sorry."

She looked up at him with shimmering eyes. Had she been about to cry? Was it because of him?

The sermon started, and she took her hand from the pew, resting it in her lap. It was only a few inches away from him, but the space felt like the farthest mountain peak. Visible, but untouchable.

He sat through the service without learning anything, for how could one learn of peace with such turmoil within? When it ended, Edna fairly dashed out of the chapel. Hugh tried to follow, but he was less nimble, and with every second the throng of churchgoers thickened.

Finally he stepped into the sunny afternoon, squinting as he cast his eyes about looking for her. She stood at the Grahams' wagon. He took one step closer, but someone caught his cuff. He turned to see Catherine smiling up at him.

"I didn't know you had such a fine voice. How come I've never heard you sing like that before?"

Hugh glanced at Edna and swallowed. Then he turned back to Catherine. What did he say? *I wasn't singing for you. I was singing for the girl I'd mistreated, a girl who means too much to a poor boy like me.* Unlike with Catherine, Edna was more than all the right things on a list. Catherine would make some man very happy. That man was never going to be Hugh.

"I have to go." He tugged free and heard a small scoff as he walked away. Edna wasn't at the wagon any longer, and his gaze swept the park in search of her. Finally he spotted her, at *his* family wagon. He took courage, hoping if he pleaded with her, she might forgive his awful treatment.

"Edna," he breathed as soon as he reached her. He didn't

dare take his eyes off her, but he hoped the family knew well enough to hang back and let him speak to her alone.

She turned, her mouth working like she wanted to say something, but couldn't find the nerve.

"I'm sorry I got angry about Lachlan's medicine." He shook his head at the memory. "I was mad at myself. I'd been coveting Garrick's life of freedom, and I felt guilty when you came and told me you'd found a solution. I was angry at myself, not at you."

"Hugh." She swallowed, as if that one word had taken all her courage.

"You have been nothing but good to my family. You're so good." His chest filled with love for this woman. He wanted to reach out, to pull her to his chest and wrap his arms around her. How could he endure being near her without his heart breaking every time?

"Hugh," she said again, more firmly.

He looked into her pale green eyes, wishing she and him were far away from this town, wishing they were riding double through a dense wood with her snuggled against his chest.

"Catherine said something, and I think she's right."

Catherine. Hugh wanted to growl the name. "I saw you two before church."

Edna reached out and hooked her first finger around Hugh's pinky. "A good man is worth fighting for."

Hugh unhooked his thumb from his pocket, and interlaced their fingers. Did she think him a good man, even after he'd spoken harshly to her? He brushed his thumb across her knuckles with a featherlight touch. Inside, he fought a battle. He wanted to reassure her, but he wouldn't be dishonest. He had to make sure she understood.

"My family will always be my responsibility. Lachlan

might be able to help, but I could never leave, never go far away in case they needed me."

"I know."

"I'll never have the money for nice things. No matter if I trapped every single night."

"I know." She placed her palm flat against his chest. "I want you by *my* side at night." Her cheeks colored then, and Hugh stepped closer.

Every voice in his head shouted that he wasn't good enough, that she would want more one day. But he finally understood Jimmy. He would rather work himself into the ground loving this woman, than watch her love anyone else.

"I can't build you a house."

Edna grinned, her eyes sparkling. "I don't mind cozy."

Hugh ran his free hand over his face, scrubbing away the image of her in his bed back home. With his family in the rooms surrounding them. He didn't want that. He wanted a life for them, not to just plug her into the life he was already living.

"I mind it. I want more for us."

She toyed with the buttons on this shirt. "Della has offered me her guest house."

The idea struck him like a bolt of lightning. She was slaying all his excuses, and he wasn't foolish enough to keep attempting to convince her. "Are you sure?"

He locked his knees, afraid if he didn't, he might get down on them and beg her to be sure. He didn't want her to take him because he'd pressured her.

"I'm not afraid of hard work. Nor am I afraid of the weight of your family. I love them, and I wanted to ease that burden long before I decided I loved you. I love you because of your commitment to them, not despite it."

It was Hugh's turn to work his mouth, searching for words.

Edna laughed. "You've made me a bit forward, cowboy. Now I'll never be able to play coy."

Hugh slid an arm around her waist and tugged her tighter against him. He met her eyes then, staring into them unabashed. "You've been coy for long enough." He gulped, nearly leaning in to kiss her, but they had an audience of at least his family. Perhaps the Grahams too, and maybe a few Prices.

He pulled away, hating the movement even as he performed it. Sliding his hand down her arm, he led her to the horse and made sure the beast's head blocked them from view. As he held her hand, he remembered every time he'd wished to do so, but had held back. She met his gaze once more, placing a careful hand on his shoulder, soft as she'd always been while tending his wound. He didn't want gentle just now. He snaked his other hand around her waist and pulled her closer. She loved him. The reality raced across his mind like a herd of mustangs, kicking up dust and obscuring everything else. He pressed his forehead to hers. "I love you, Edna. I have for far too long."

Releasing her hand, he brought his palm up and entwined his fingers in her hair. Leaning in, he pressed his lips to hers.

She surrendered to him then, in a way that he'd longed for since that first dance when he'd had to force himself away. He'd kept forcing distance between them after that, because he had known, even then, that this woman had the potential to bring him to his knees.

———

HIS LIPS WERE ON HERS, silky and urgent. Lady whinnied and Edna couldn't stop the laugh that bubbled out. They broke apart, but Edna held his tight. "You've scandalized your horse."

She raised onto her toes and tried to look out at the congregation on the lawn. She wasn't tall enough to see anything, but Hugh still pulled her back to him.

"I love you." He said again, his voice low.

The words spread like butter on hot bread, sinking into all the holes. When she'd decided to tell him she loved him, she'd also decided it didn't matter if he didn't return her love, or if he never said it back. For love wasn't something that was only given in fair amounts. When you loved someone, it didn't matter if they loved you back.

She'd given Brandon much more love than he'd ever returned. That didn't mean her love was any cheaper. But she was glad now to know she was giving it to someone worthy.

She faked a glare. "It took you long enough to say it."

"I fell for you at that first dance."

Edna chuckled. "Don't flatter me. You fairly ran away from me."

"Precisely."

Edna blinked at him, trying to remember it again but this time from a different angle. "You spent the evening with Catherine."

Hugh shrugged. "She's been my friend for a long time. I spent many dances near her and the rest of my friends."

"She doesn't think you two are friends. She's waiting for you. Probably wishing she could turn me into a pillar of salt." Perhaps she had heard more of the sermon than she thought.

"I've told her more than once that I don't intend to marry."

"She's willing to wait." After their little chat, Edna was certain.

Hugh sighed.

Edna hated herself for pushing away this man when she'd just got hold of him, but Catherine deserved clarity. "Speak to her."

Hugh came back and pressed a kiss to her lips, then moved away before Edna was ready. She clung to Lady's head and stroked her nose as she watched the man she loved walk toward his childhood sweetheart. Looking into the horse's eye, Edna said, "I should be a bit embarrassed, but I'm still a broken music box. I don't know how to play a tune the right way. I guess it doesn't matter, so long as all the notes get played by the end."

Fay came around the wagon with a smirk on her face. "Absolute scandal," she whispered with a laugh.

Edna bit her bottom lip. "Can I ever show my face in town again?"

Fay considered. "Only with Hugh at your side for protection. I know all too well how vicious the Price women can be."

Edna sighed. "I didn't want to hurt anyone."

"Nobody is good enough for them. I doubt Hugh would have made the cut in the long run."

Edna remembered what Catherine had said about Jimmy and his wife. "She told me about Jimmy."

Fay's face was solemn as she nodded. "Worked himself into the ground trying to please his wife. I don't doubt that's the very reason Hugh has resisted Catherine all these years."

"He thought Catherine would want more eventually." As she said it, it was like a key fitting perfectly in a lock she'd never been able to see the inner workings of. Hugh, eternally afraid of disappointing his wife, of her not being content with his family situation. "And I went and tried to *help* him be free of Lachlan's medicine." His anger made sense now, and his apology more of a contradiction. "But what changed his mind?"

"Maybe the tongue-lashing I gave him."

Edna smiled. "You didn't."

Fay shook her head. "I'm teasing. He didn't need it. You

should have seen him all last week. I haven't seen him that bad since Lachlan's diagnosis."

"I meant to help."

Fay laid a hand on Edna's arm. "You did. We are all so grateful. I hope Hugh has told you so now, since he sure didn't last week."

Edna blushed at things both said and unsaid.

Mrs. Morris and Lachlan climbed into the seat of the wagon. Mrs. Morris leaned toward Edna. "Your ride is loading up, and I think it best if you weren't stuck in town today."

She cut a glance to Hugh and Catherine. Edna followed the path to see Catherine slap Hugh. In a twirl of fabric and lace she stomped away. Edna's stomach clenched, for as glad as she was that Hugh had finally set Catherine straight, Edna had never been inclined to take pleasure in another's pain.

She climbed into the back of the Morris' wagon, catching Della's eye and giving her friend a nod. Della returned it, which at least meant Della knew Edna had her own ride to the valley and would be able to make her way to the ranch.

Edna sat on the side of the wagon so she faced the gathering crowd. She felt several eyes on her, and not just the ones belonging to a Price. Hugh climbed in and sat beside her. She took his hand, and they faced the crowd together as Lachlan drove them away from the wide-eyed gossips.

As soon as they were out of sight, Edna relaxed into Hugh. "You're lucky she was wearing gloves."

Hugh's chest shook as he chuckled. "Do you know much about slapping men?"

Truthfully, she only knew about clapping her own hands together, but she did know a bit about being slapped. It had only happened once, and it had been when Edna had tried defending Frederick. She gulped. She didn't want to tell

Hugh about those darker days. She wanted to allow her life to start at this moment.

She straightened and met his gaze, holding it until he lost the humor in his face. "You have to love me."

His brows pulled together, and he opened his mouth, but she gave his hand a squeeze. "I'm not done." She swallowed, collecting her thoughts. "I know we will fight, and we might even raise our voices, but you have to love me the same before and after. You can't just love me because you're sorry for what you did."

He released her hand and gripped her shoulders. "I would never do that."

"Promise."

He nodded. "I promise."

She stared at him for a moment, trying to sense any weakness. Trying to discern whether any person could guarantee what she was asking. When she decided he meant it true, she sat back and leaned her head against his shoulder once more. Fay sat at the front of the wagon, talking with her mama. Edna smiled at her friend's attempt to give Edna and Hugh a sliver of privacy.

With her free hand, Edna tickled the back of his fingers. "What promise do you want from me?" She glanced up, and he shook his head.

She sat up and faced him once more. "Nothing?"

He shook it again, a silly grin on his face.

"What about a promise to be content?"

He gripped her hand. "No."

"You don't want me to be content?"

"That's not something you can promise me. I would hate to think you weren't truthful with me in an attempt to keep a promise."

Edna nodded. "I promise to love your family as my own, to help them the way I helped my mama."

He pressed his lips together and closed his eyes. "I love you, Edna Archer."

"I love you, too." Even though they had no horse head to hide behind, she pulled him close and pressed her lips to his. Softer than that first time, more of a surrender, and she knew she wanted this man to surrender everything to her. She wanted to share his burdens, to love what he loved. To dream his dreams. To sleep in his arms. It didn't matter if they lived in a shabby cabin with a too-small stove, or in that tiny house with his family. She would be content with him at her side.

EPILOGUE

FAY FUSSED with Edna's hair, complimenting the color, then tugging at it like she loathed every strand.

Edna watched Fay's face in the mirror, but didn't dare ask her friend about Garrick, not when Fay had Edna's hair in her hands and each strand was so tenderly connected to Edna's scalp. Mama bustled in, followed closely by Mrs. Morris.

"Everyone is ready." Mama ran her hand along Edna's dress, which was hanging in the closet, cleaned and pressed. Lydia and Edna had made it from a bolt of beautiful deep blue fabric they'd purchased in town. It was plain enough to be worn every day, but, for now, it was new.

Edna turned to Fay. "Do you think Catherine will be here?"

Fay smiled. "You didn't hear? She eloped. A soldier in Worthington."

Edna blinked, first at the drama, and then she smiled. "She really was waiting for Hugh." But Fay was not smiling. Had the soldier reminded Fay of Garrick? Would her friend ever recover from those few days with that man? Edna knew better than most how quickly one's life could be altered, how strong feelings could form in an instant.

Fay shook her head and sighed. "Are you sure you want to marry my brother? He knows little about women."

Edna stood, unbuttoning her dress so she could step into her new gown. "He only needs to know about one woman." She winked at Fay and accepted her gown from Mama.

Once she was dressed and ready, she followed Mrs. Morris and her mama from the parsonage to the front doors of the church. As she walked, Edna caught Mrs. Morris' hand and pressed her fingers. Hugh's mama glanced at Edna and gave her a sad smile.

This morning, Mr. Morris had woken with such a cough that he stayed in bed with a poultice on his chest—one of Pete's special blends. Edna wasn't sure that man wasn't a wizard, for Hugh hadn't needed a doctor either. She only hoped Mr. Morris would be well soon. The worry in Mrs. Morris' face tugged at Edna's heart.

Fay and Mrs. Morris stepped forward to open the church doors while Mama acted as Edna's escort. The windows behind the dais lit up the space and created a halo effect on her husband-to be, who stood to the left of the pastor.

She blushed at his huge grin, glancing around to see if anyone else saw, but they had eyes only for her. Her cheeks flamed as Mama led her down the aisle and deposited her in front of Hugh. Edna held no flowers, and as she wrung her fingers, she understood that was why brides carried them— to hide their nerves. It was silly, she knew, for everyone here already knew she was besotted with this man, and he loved her equally in return.

He took her hands, stilling them in his warm grip. Those hands that were quick with a trigger, yet gentle when he had removed her soggy boot and wrapped her frozen foot. She realized those boots hadn't been fit for the west long before she'd ruined them traipsing through the forest. They'd been a bad fit ever since she'd left Chicago, perhaps before.

The boots she wore now had been purchased in Dragonfly Creek, and though they had no embellishments, they were sturdy and built for life out west. They had a square toe box, and her toes had room to move instead of being pinched all the time for vanity's sake. These boots promised longevity and comfort. They were made to fit her, rather than her enduring discomfort and numbness to fit into them.

She smiled at the man she loved standing across from her and thought his love for her was much the same. No need to change her shape to fit his love. His love allowed her to move and grow and *be*. Her smile widened, and Hugh gave her a quizzical grin in return. She would tell him about the thought later, for the pastor had started speaking, and Edna tried her best to listen to the words instead of ogle her soon-to-be husband.

WHEN EVERYONE HAD FINALLY CLEARED from the guesthouse, Edna went to the bed and put her feet up. Hugh joined her with a basket in his hands.

She sat up. "What's this?"

"Just a little something from my family."

Edna screwed up her face. "They're mine now, too."

Hugh chuckled. "Should I call them The Family?"

She scrunched her nose. "You make them sound like something to be avoided."

He sat on the bed and set the basket in her lap. A square of folded gingham fabric hid its contents. Edna lifted each corner, letting light into the darkness. The first thing her eyes snagged on was a pistol. She lifted her gaze to Hugh. "A gun? Perhaps I don't know your family as well as I thought. *Are* they to be avoided?"

Hugh took the gun from the basket with a smile.

Edna leaned away from the cruel instrument.

"It doesn't have any lead in it." He popped the inner compartment out to show her it was empty. "It's something my papa did for Eloise, and when he learned you didn't have one, he insisted."

"It's too much." Edna shook her head, knowing what it must have cost them to purchase.

Hugh set it back in the basket. "You're part of The Family now. And besides, I'd say you earned it. It's one of the pistols I took off the bandits."

She eyed the weapon with new understanding. Part of her wanted nothing to do with something that had been used for such cruel deeds, but the pistol held her memories too and she was glad to have it.

With a nod, she picked up the next item. Several scraps of colored fabric sewn together like a banner. "Is this The Family flag?"

Hugh laughed. "Perhaps. Mama said she's making us a wedding quilt. She said that will give you an idea of what it will look like."

Edna clutched the fabric to her chest, tears burning the back of her eyes. "We were looking at scraps for a quilt. I thought your mama was just asking my opinion, but she was asking for this. How did she know?"

Hugh waggled his eyebrows. "Are you sure you're ready to learn The Family's secrets?"

Edna threw the fabric at him. "Stop *saying* it like that!"

He laughed and handed her the next two items in the basket. Two large, hand-carved wooden spoons.

"From Lachlan and me both."

Edna leaned forward and kissed him, so filled with love

she wanted to stay there forever, opening this bountiful basket of most thoughtful gifts.

When they broke apart, she ran her thumb along one of the spoon's rounded edges, still rough from being carved so recently.

Hugh tapped the end of one. "I'll sand them smoother before we use them."

Edna set them down and looked inside again, but nothing else remained.

Hugh smirked. "Fay said her present was taking Garrick the wrong way and giving us an extra day to fall in love."

Edna burst out laughing, the emotion from the day and this gift pouring out of her.

When she settled, she pulled him close. "I can't tell you how glad I am to be part of your family." And she hoped he heard her, that he believed she didn't want anything to be different.

"The Family," he corrected, kissing her once, twice, then several times more.

ALSO BY KATE CONDIE

Want free content and more from Kate Condie? Sign up for her newsletter at www.subscribepage.com/katecondienewsletter or follow her on social media @authorkatecondie

ACKNOWLEDGMENTS

Thank you to my family for supporting me as I write this series. To the kids for keeping quiet and to Cody for keeping them so.

As always my team is amazing. To Michelle for being my alpha reader and brainstorm buddy. For listening while I changed the plot a thousand times. To Whitney with Empowered Writing for your incredible line editing skills. You make editing an absolute joy. To Kari with CookieLynn publishing for your quick and complete copy edit. Also to my proofreaders and champions, Beth with Magnolia Author services, Ariel, and Taryn. Then to Raneé with Sweetly Us for the amazing covers she always creates, and dealing with my ridiculous indecisiveness. You are all such shining stars in this world of writing. Thank you!

Lastly, I want to thank you, dear readers. You buy my books and it baffles me to see my work being read in countries across the globe. You leave reviews that tell me you get these characters and you love immersing yourself in this imaginary world. Your enjoyment and support keeps me publishing these books. Because of you, I get to turn my hobby into a job and I'm forever grateful for that opportunity.

ABOUT THE AUTHOR

Kate Condie is a speed talker from Oregon. Reading has been part of her life since childhood, where she devoured everything from mysteries, to classics, to nonfiction—and of course, romance. At first, her writing was purely journal format as she thought writing novels was for the lucky ones. She lives in Utah and spends her days surrounded by mountains with her favorite hunk, their four children and her laptop. In her free time she reads, tries to learn a host of new instruments, binge watches anything by BBC and tries to keep up with Lafayette as she sings the Hamilton soundtrack.

CPSIA information can be obtained
at www.ICGtesting.com
Printed in the USA
LVHW102347161122
733184LV00008B/326